ROMEO'S BEAT

VINCENT ATCHITY

STORY MERCHANT BOOKS
LOS ANGELES
2021

Story Merchant Books
400 S. Burnside Avenue #11B
Los Angeles, CA 90036

www.storymerchantbooks.com

Interior format & cover design by IndieDesignz.com

For 99 8 days a week

No está la cosa en pensar mucho, sino en amar mucho.
                                    —Teresa of Avila

Therwyth she was alway so trewe
Our joye was ever ylyche newe;
Oure hertes wern so evene a payre
That never nas that oon contrayre
To that other for no woo.
                                    —Geoffrey Chaucer

Our birth is but a sleep and a forgetting;
The Soul that rises with us, our life's Star,
Hath had elsewhere its setting
And cometh from afar;
Not in entire forgetfulness,
And not in utter nakedness,
But trailing clouds of glory do we come.
                                    —William Wordsworth

PROLOGUE

Juliet Sawyer was down on her hands and knees in the far corner of the garden. The late autumn sun was unexpectedly hot on her back, and she could feel a tiny rivulet of perspiration trickling down her neck and into her blouse. She was weeding. Choosing one life over another with practiced fingers had become one of her favorite activities. Visitors always admired the tidiness of her garden, but she knew better. However merciless her culling, it wouldn't take much more than a week of rain when spring came for the native prairie grasses to start to emerge again among the perennial herbs. Their hunger for life would call her back to her hands and knees again and again throughout the growing season to be the agent of death.

Not that Juliet had any objection to the prairie grasses. Unlike most of the folks who lived in the deliberately ordered suburban world of Prairie Village, Juliet, the botanist, had taken a keen interest in the Kansas grasslands. The plants that settlers and farmers had battled since the earliest days of the pioneers had seeded the plains for thousands of years. A century of repression meant nothing to them. Layer upon layer, the soil had been deeply sown with a more ancient history, and every spring the grasses were ready to reclaim their dominion when she relaxed her vigilance for more than a few days.

The grasses that she pulled while weeding her garden were impossible for most eyes to distinguish from one another, but Juliet had come to know them. She had also come to have a deep feeling of appreciation for their persistence and permanence in the landscape, as well as for the brevity of her own persistence in plucking them. She knew the native grasses would outlast this garden and these fingers of hers. This was an unexpected comfort.

Juliet often drove out to the Prairie Center in Olathe, the four hundred or so acres that, amidst thousands of miles of cultivation, had been allowed to return to a near natural state. Those four hundred acres were the nearest thing to wilderness that she had found in the state of Kansas. Juliet was fairly certain that those open acres were the only reason that she'd been able to go on living contentedly in this part of the world for as long as she had. Order was important to her. All it took was a single glance at her garden to see that she believed in the sort of beauty that could only be brought about by deliberate culling and cultivation. But to thrive, Juliet knew that she, her daughter, and her garden depended on a depth of soil that was wild beyond her invention or control.

She'd dedicated the other side of the backyard to the original grasses. Not that she'd just let them come up any which way. The truly wild was not an aesthetic that was compatible with a suburban backyard. But she'd been one of the nation's leading innovators in native plant landscaping. She grew big bluestem, switchgrass, side-oats grama, and prairie cordgrass in a carefully plotted arrangement that displayed their varying colors and heights to an advantage that never failed to impress, and that had won her recognition in two different local women's magazines and a prize from the Prairie Village Chamber of Commerce. She took as much, or more, satisfaction in that local acknowledgement as she'd ever taken from her publications in academic journals and in *Architectural Design,* or the awards she'd received from national horticultural societies.

Weeding and clearing debris in preparation for winter and for the spring which always followed, Juliet knew, were the vital uncelebrated tasks of a gardener. After all had been planned and sown, the work that remained was the regular maintenance of the frontier that separated order from chaos.

She paused and used the back of her wrist to push a strand of hair from her forehead, leaving a smudge of earth there. She thought, as she had so many times before, that weeding was one of the activities that made her feel human, in the best and most fundamental sense of the word.

As her practiced fingers selected and removed each upstart, she gave quiet thanks for her awareness of the present moment and of all of the movements and dimensions that intersected to form it. Juliet was present, aware, and grateful. It had become her steady state of being after long, difficult ages of emotional tossing and heaving and feeling like she was being held under by the tremendous weight of regrets and futile pleadings.

Juliet had come to rest in the old truth that we are here to be gardeners. We find our meaning in loving the wild life of the earth, and in using our intelligence and discipline and sweat of our brows to seek a healthy and sustainable balance between cultivated order and the endless profusion that is the wellspring of all life. At the age of forty-one, Juliet felt like a strong tree that had sunk its roots deep and borne good fruit—through all the harshness of conditions and twisting pursuit of light.

She was pulling the sturdy intrusions of buffalo grass that had come up between her rosemary and her thyme. It had been a week since the last rain, and the sun-warmed herbs were at their most fragrant. As she pulled and picked, she could hear the sweet sound of the best fruit she'd borne. Hearing her daughter Gloria singing more beautifully than ever magnified beyond all measure the joy that Juliet found in her simple task.

There had been a time, not so long ago, when Gloria had liked nothing more than to join her mother in the garden on the weekends. They had years and years together, living in a garden-like little world of simplest things. Putting shoes on to go outside and get muddy. Trying out all the tools, putting them to all the wrong purposes. Dancing and singing to make the rain come, and shivering together under a blanket on the sofa when the thunder cracked overhead and made their house shake.

From the very beginning and at every age, Gloria immersed Juliet in the healing flow of presence. Seasons of denial, anger, and sorrow had turned to revolving seasons of unexpected and stunning joys. Her heart had mended and become as stout as an oak, and as big as the whole wide world.

Juliet supposed that there might come a time in some remote future when Gloria would want to kneel beside her again to weed. But now, at the age of seventeen, what Gloria did was dance, sing, and spend hours at the piano working on her unique compositions with amazing focus. She never failed to bless her mother with smiles and hugs, before spinning and pulling away again to return to her music. Juliet was grateful to find herself, unexpectedly, strong enough for this season of separation, too.

She inhaled deeply, filling her head with the fragrance of warm thyme. All of her garden smells held deep associations for her, but especially this one.

She grew three different kinds of thyme, but just one of them was the descendant of the handful of cuttings that she had smuggled back into the country with her after a visit to a particular hillside above the Río Tormes almost two decades ago. She liked to imagine that the tough little perennial in the corner of her Kansas garden could trace its heritage back to the Romans who carried it north with them from the Mediterranean.

The return and growth of that thyme, year after year, was one of her chief satisfactions. And all she'd done was put it in the ground. Life could be so tenacious. It had nothing to do with her.

Working with the earth had taught Juliet to view her memories as the soil from which her present self reached up towards the sun. They glowed inside her, warming her from within, empowering her to stretch and grow. As she turned the soil in her garden, she allowed herself to revisit scenes from the past that otherwise remained deep inside her. She remembered long warm nights that turned into mornings, and she remembered not wanting or needing to sleep.

They had crushed thyme with every footstep. He had held her in the grass by the side of a nameless tarn that was dark gray and brightest blue like the mixed sky above them. She remembered the ancient smell of the interior of twelfth century churches, and it merged with the loamy aroma that she coaxed out of the ground with her fingers.

When Gloria's voice reached her ears again Juliet sat up on her heels abruptly. Sure enough, there it came again. *Sunshine and thyme on the empty hill above the silent city we're dancing still.*

"Sunshine & Thyme", the 1985 hit by Romeo's Beat, had been a constant throughout Gloria's increasingly musical childhood. But Juliet had never heard her sing it quite like this. Full-throated, with every inflection perfect, it was more than homage, it was like a prayer, or a voice from another world.

It was uncanny. With a catch in her throat, and a tear in her eye that felt as good as the sun on the back of her hands and as clean as the soil under her nails, Juliet was overcome by a rushing sensation as nearly twenty years collapsed away to nothing.

She tried to sing the verse herself, but found that she was having trouble breathing. Her voice cracked and fell, and she felt tears welling up in her eyes. Hoping now that her daughter wouldn't come out to the garden and find her weeping, Juliet dug both her hands into the soil and remembered the afternoon she'd looked up from her postcards and caught Colin Hogan staring at her.

1

The overnight Paris-Madrid train crossed the Spanish border and stopped in Irún just as day was turning to dusk. The air coming through the compartment's open window smelled of cold sea and moist pine. Outside, the green hillside below the station ran through the village right down to the water's edge.

Once he was sure that the train wouldn't be departing from Irún until seven twenty-five, and that he really had two hours to explore, Colin Hogan pulled his gray backpack down from the overhead rack, slung it over his shoulders, then reached for his broad-brimmed hat and his white guitar.

It was the summer of 1984. Colin had been moving from place to place for nearly three months, and was traveling lightly. His backpack wasn't as stuffed as it could have been. He liked to be able to close all the zippers without a struggle, and so had room to spare when he set out from L.A. in mid-April.

He was wearing faded jeans, and lace-up leather boots. His gray button-front shirt was tucked in loosely, and his long sleeves were rolled up almost to his elbows. His thick chestnut-colored hair hung in long locks that nearly reached his shoulders.

He stepped onto the station platform, and clapped his big weather-stained hat on his head to keep his hair back out of his eyes. Five young women were waiting together on the platform. They were all staring at him. He winked at them, touched the peak of his hat in a nineteenth-century gesture, and smiled as he crossed the platform and opened the door to the tiny station house. The women giggled and whispered to each other and stared after him as he went.

Tall, slender, well-muscled, with the beautiful head of hair, and deep blue eyes, Colin was often admired for his looks. And there was something about the way his eyes flashed around sharply and then held on warmly to what they found. With his backpack and guitar, and with the rugged adventurer's hat on his head, he stood out plainly as a traveler. But, he didn't look like the other youthful backpackers who were criss-crossing Europe in such numbers that summer. For one thing, Colin didn't easily give himself away as an American. Women who looked up because they wanted to see the face that went with the cool boots, found that they'd keep on looking because of something mysterious about his origin and his destination.

It was hard to tell Colin's age, too, and this made them wonder all the more. His unblemished skin and his long energetic stride made his youth apparent. But the way he looked at things, and the way he sometimes stopped in his tracks, as if listening to something of remote and subtle beauty, made it clear that he relished time and detail with the wisdom of one who knows that our time on earth is short.

As he left the station and began to make his way down the busy street, Colin kept his ears tuned to the voices of his fellow pedestrians, and to the sound of the music that emerged from the doorways of bars. In France and then in England, he'd discovered that live music was as much of a rarity in Europe as it was at home. Video jukeboxes were the new thing that summer, and most of the bars had one. In the places that didn't, recorded music--whether from single media jukeboxes, or from cassette tapes, or radio--still ruled. And, from what Colin was hearing now as he made his way down a Spanish street for the first time, he might have been anywhere else in the world.

Before leaving home, Colin had heard that culture had become homogenized worldwide. But he hadn't really understood what that meant until he'd arrived in France and found nearly the same top-forty playing there, too. In love with the simplicity of computer-generated beats and rhythms, many bands had been trimmed down to creative twosomes, and it seemed like a lot of musicians had lost interest in instruments.

Still, luminous exceptions abounded. Colin's ears were crowded with sounds that he knew would outlast the summer. The high, ringing guitar sound that The Edge produced for U2, for example, never ceased to grab his attention, no matter how often he heard it singing out of a jukebox. Richard Butler's voice, or Robert Smith's voice and guitar, and now this Cyndi Lauper!—these were sounds that made Colin shiver with anxiety and delight. He knew that they would go on living far beyond their decade. Colin understood that just because people listened to whatever music was available in the moment, it didn't mean that people weren't hungry for music they'd love forever.

2

On the basis of a demo tape that he'd made with a few of his friends, Colin had gotten the attention of a record producer in Hollywood. He'd been offered, and had signed, a contract. He'd been assigned studio time. Three days before they were scheduled to go in, Colin had called it off.

The guys in his band had freaked. But Colin was the driver: music and lyrics were all his. His bassist and his keyboard player tried to reason with him, then got angry, and then they'd just walked out. The drummer, who'd known him the longest, had punctuated their departure with a rumble and cymbal crash.

"You gotta do what you gotta do, huh, Colin?" he'd said with a shrug. "I'll be here for you. You get this right, you'll be doing it for all of us."

Colin didn't just want a recording contract, unlike so many short-sighted musicians. He knew that his music and lyrics were both good, better than a lot of the stuff that was being produced. He also knew that most of what was recorded never made it to the radio, and that radio play was all that mattered. Colin didn't even just want a hit, which was what the A&R guys for the label wanted. What he wanted was radio play that would go on playing. He wanted a sound that would last. There was still stuff from the fifties, sixties, and seventies on the radio. He wanted his songs to make it to the next generation.

The guy who'd signed him had laughed in his face when he explained all of this. Stevie Kassabian was no newcomer to the music business. He was in his mid-forties, but still dressed the way he had when he'd gotten his first job with the label during the Summer of Love. He had a frizzy gray afro, a long mustache, wore bell-bottomed jeans and clogs, and left his paisley-patterned silk shirt unbuttoned most of the way down his chest. Colin just stared at the curls of graying chest hair that vibrated with the man's laughter, thinking that the other guys had been right, and that it was all over.

"Man, I can't tell you how many times I've heard that crap about making a sound that will last. You don't think everyone wants that? Well, let me tell you: everyone wants that. You don't think I want that for you? Well, let me tell you: I want that for you. Hell, man. I want that for *me*. So, it isn't the first time I've heard it. But it's definitely the first time I've heard someone tell *me* that *they* want to cancel their recording date because they're not sure they have the sound right. That's my job, you know? I'm the one who tells you you're not ready. I'm the one who lets you down, as easy as I can. So this is something new. You're too much, baby."

Stevie Kassabian had grown up in Brooklyn, and talked fast. Outrageous, he'd become the source of all record producer stereotypes. Now Stevie suddenly became silent, and stayed silent. For a long couple of minutes, the only sound in the gold-record lined office was the noise from the traffic on Sunset Boulevard four stories below. Then, Stevie shook his head slowly, and exhaled with a long whistling sound.

"So, we'll reschedule. You want to record in six months? We'll book studio time in six months. It's not like there won't still be a music business in six months. Who the hell am I, anyway? I could tell you it's just a crap shoot with impossible odds. I could tell you that there's no way to plan for a sound that will last. Some songs hit, some really good songs don't. Some hits seem to last forever, some really good tunes are gone from the airwaves in three months. You think four months are going to help you improve the odds? Who the hell am I to tell you they're not, huh? Who the hell am I, right?"

Colin shrugged, gratefully. Then Kassabian's face got all serious.

"Music is a lot like love, you know? The surest way of making either one of them last is by dying while you're still hot. But it doesn't work if you haven't recorded it yet, you know what I'm saying? But, who the hell am I to tell you that, right? Just don't die before you cut the record."

3

A light rain was beginning to fall, and the Irún sidewalk was crowded. As dusk began to turn to night, people were making their way home. Carrying briefcases, and grocery bags, and long loaves of bread, they now paused, in a kind of syncopated choreography, to open umbrellas. Colin imagined it all set to music, blending the gentle rise of a string section in with the ambient sounds of shoes on pavement, a fanfare of automobile horns, and the gentle murmur of snatches of conversation.

The overture ended abruptly with a squeal of brakes, and a clattering sound.

A woman approaching him on the sidewalk, plainly an alto, sang "¡Ay, la paloma!" loudly and mournfully, in perfect pitch.

Colin followed her sorrowful gaze and his eyes discovered the source of the clattering sound. A perfectly white pigeon—¡ay, la paloma!—had been struck by a passing car, and now lay in the gutter, fluttering, a broad fan of immaculate white feathers and three perfect splashes of deep red blood. An eddy formed in the pedestrian traffic as people swerved to avoid the awful scene. A few others drew closer to...do what? Help, somehow? Colin didn't know, and didn't want to think.

He turned right at the corner, his head suddenly filled with the plaintive chorus of *Cucurrucucu paloma* and a memory of reading Hemingway's *Death in the Afternoon* while sitting on a beach. He whispered *España* to himself with a shiver of excitement and imagined reaching out to squeeze the arm of his traveling companion.

She would have seen what he'd seen, and felt a whole rush of different feelings and associations that they could share now, adding layers of rich dimension to the cinematic moment and engraving it permanently in the memory they were building together.

What she looked like had changed over time. For a considerable stretch, he had pictured her as a willowy, outdoorsy blonde with brown eyes. That vision had been based on a girl who'd sat across from him for a year during a high school history class, with whom he'd never dared to exchange even a word.

Lately, what she looked like had pretty much stopped mattering. He caught little glimpses of her in women of all different shapes and sizes, based not on their appearances but on flashes and moments of recognition, or imagined understandings.

Once, in Arles, he'd exchanged smiles with a young woman with wet black hair who was walking towards him across the plaza when they both overheard a young boy telling his younger brother that the sun is a big ball of hot gas and a star. Then, as they passed by each other, he caught the warm, floral smell of her shampoo and felt for a few minutes utterly bereft as he strode on alone.

As the days turned into weeks, and he left France for Ireland, and then England, his perfect companion had no trouble leaving one culture behind with him and quickly and completely engaging with the next. Ireland's verdant hillsides filled her with hilarious joy as she ran down them alongside of him, falling, and lying back in the rich green grass. Together they fell in love with the immense trees in the Magdalen College gardens at Oxford.

She could hear what he'd heard in the odd sounds he tried to coax from his guitar, and didn't at all mind that he sometimes liked to sit up late singing imperfect things, stringing words together. She had her own pursuits. They'd spend long quiet afternoons together, companionable and distinct, each following the dictates of a different muse.

She shared her deepest, most passionate thoughts with him as they arose, without checking herself, knowing he'd listen, knowing he'd see. She reached out to squeeze his arm, to be sure he didn't miss a thing.

But Colin's perfect traveling companion was purely imaginary. She always had been.

He'd had a string of girlfriends. He had taken trips with two of them.

He'd spent ten days driving from San Francisco to New York with Eva, the girl he'd dated for a year and a half in college. As students, they'd been good company for each other. The fact that Eva was two years ahead of him didn't make any difference. They both took their studies seriously and shared an interest in music. After late nights in the library, Colin walked Eva home through the sketchy Berkeley streets to her slightly beat student apartment and as often as not, reluctant to let the moment pass, she'd invite him to come up to her room to listen to some new album that she'd picked up at Rasputin.

The music, the lateness of the hour, and the intimacy of her small candle-lit room led them into each other's arms. They made love in a weary kind of late night solipsism, and Colin got up and headed out into the street again at first light so that Eva wouldn't get grief from her two housemates for violating the house rule of no men during the peak morning bathroom hour. This seemed like a reasonable rule, and Colin came to associate Rasputin with sex, and sex with an early morning walk through empty streets lined with sun-brilliant morning glories and bougainvillea.

When Eva graduated, she asked him to help her drive home to New York. Three days into the trip, she'd kicked him out of their tent at dawn. Colin had been lying there, wide awake, listening to the solitary cry of a bird he'd never heard before, and wondering about the last stars of the night.

"You want to get up and get out there," she'd said. "And I want to get some more sleep and then wake up alone. So, let's stop lying here in the mornings together and pretending we're some kind of happily married couple. You're gorgeous and it's been fun, and now we're on a road trip, and then it'll be good-bye. Or were you thinking you were going to follow me to law school? Somehow, I just don't see you spending the winter in New Jersey."

4

When they were just a half a day's drive from the end of their trip, Colin called home to check in while Eva filled the tank. His sister Clara answered, and in an uncharacteristically subdued voice she'd told him their mother had died.

Eva showed her tenderer side when she found Colin standing in the phone booth, still clutching the receiver in his hand even after he and Clara had been disconnected. She found a travel agency in the small Pennsylvania town where they'd stopped, and arranged for Colin's flight home out of JFK later that night. And then she'd driven the rest of the way to New York with one hand on his knee, while Colin sat and stared vacantly out at the traffic and the passing countryside. By the time she'd left him at the airport, she was even encouraging him to fly back out and join her as soon as he was ready.

Colin was in mid-flight somewhere over Wyoming when his father took two over-the-counter sleeping pills to help beat the insomnia that had been threatening to wipe him out in the midst of his wife's funeral arrangements. According to the doctors, the fact that he'd had two glasses of wine earlier in the evening shouldn't have made any difference. All they could say, finally, was that his heart must have been tired.

Both of them were fifty-five years old. They'd been high school sweethearts, and had been married for thirty-two years. Whenever Colin thought about them afterwards, he pictured them in the kitchen together, laughing, his mother with a wine glass in her hand and his father wearing the silly toque that she'd given him for his birthday.

Given their age, good health, and excellent spirits, neither parent had thought to plan for a tragedy of this magnitude. What little life insurance there was enabled Colin and Clara to pay off the mortgage on the family home in Albany. When school opened again at the end of the summer, Clara was going to begin her freshman year at Mills College and Colin was going to be a junior at Cal. They fought about it bitterly, but in the end Colin prevailed.

He withdrew from the university and took an entry-level job at a bank so that he could help Clara with her tuition and other expenses. The metronomic routine of the work at the bank, though as dull as it could possibly be, helped him to focus on his music. He wrote in the early mornings, before putting on the required shirt and tie. In the evenings, he played the guitar for hours.

Every evening when Clara returned home from class or the library, she opened the door to the sound of her brother's playing. She made dinner for the two of them, and then they moved to the living room where Clara did her studying while Colin went on with his practice and composition. She promised herself that as soon as she graduated, she'd give him whatever time he needed to finish his studies, or do whatever he wanted to do.

5

The rain was coming down steadily now. Colin bought an *El País* at a kiosk in the middle of the sidewalk, and then he smelled olive oil and garlic. Somebody was playing a guitar and singing in a low, guttural voice. Colin shook the rain off his hat, and stepped inside the bar.

The small space was crowded with dark-haired people wearing dark clothes. They were involved in quiet conversations, or just sitting and listening. A toothless old man was playing his guitar in the corner with hands that looked like they'd grown on a tree. No one did more than glance up at Colin as he managed to take a seat at the bar without clobbering anyone with his backpack.

"*¿Qué quieres tomar?*" The bartender was a youngish man with a receding hairline, who nodded at him in friendly greeting.

"*Cerveza, por favor*," Colin answered. The grill behind the bar was busy with six rows of mushrooms sizzling with oil, garlic, and parsley. "*Y champiñones.*"

The bartender nodded. "*Champiñones a la planxa. Muy bien.*"

Colin propped his *El País* on the edge of the bar and scanned the headlines. He'd developed the habit of carrying a local paper into bars and restaurants while he was in France, as he'd found that it sometimes led the locals to indulge his halting efforts to communicate a bit longer than they seemed to otherwise. But being able to read the paper with this degree of ease was a welcome novelty. It felt like one of his senses had been restored after long impairment.

The beer was icy cold. The *champiñones* were still sizzling when they were delivered to him on a small plate with toothpicks stuck in them. Garlic and parsley floated in tiny pools of oil in the center of each one.

Colin had learned to cook from his father, and had a deep appreciation for simple dishes that brought together fundamental elements. The smell of olive oil and garlic had won him over before he'd even realized its source. It had grabbed at something inside him that was older than he was, something that was inside everyone, and that would outlast any individual. For lyrics to last, Colin thought, they needed to incorporate something as fundamental as olive oil and garlic.

Colin ate one of the mushrooms. *Exquisito.* The word swam up out of his memory. He was in Spain, and it was like he'd arrived home in some kind of parallel universe.

But as Colin sat and ate and listened, he realized that Spanish was not the language of the house. There were bits of Spanish in the air, but the dominant tongue was one he'd never heard before. Some of the tone and intonation was similar to Spanish, and the vowels seemed to be the same. But the language was richly populated with guttural t's, d's, and k's and long words that took unexpected turns.

It was Euskera, the prehistoric language of the Basque country. Colin was more at home than he'd been in weeks and weeks, and at the very same time he was in more utterly alien territory than he'd ever been. He felt a thrill run through him, and again imagined reaching over to squeeze the arm of his companion. She'd be feeling the topsy-turvy peculiarity of it all, too, and it would be something that they'd both remember and talk about in detail years later in places of their own that they'd have made familiar.

The second time he'd traveled with a woman had been when the bass player from his first band had asked him to accompany her to

Seattle. Gretchen was her name, and she'd been invited to play a show with some friends of hers over the Fourth of July weekend. Gretchen was a talented musician, who had studied at the Berklee College of Music in Boston. As band members, they were constantly butting heads. Gretchen's formal training often led her to object to Colin's creative impulses. She called him a naïf and a dropout. He called her a bluestocking.

The music they made together reflected their differences. Jarring, angry, and discordant, it appealed to a small punk-era audience at the late night gigs they played. The tension between them during rehearsals was magnified into a minor electrical storm when they were on stage. Post-performance, they'd often wind up, hot and sweaty, in each other's arms. On more than one occasion, Gretchen punctuated the evening by thumping Colin on the chest with her small sharp fist and telling him that he was the best she'd ever had.

During their two-day drive up to Washington, they'd alternately argued bitterly and spent hours sitting in sullen silence. It was plain to Colin that Gretchen was fiercely attached to him, but what he knew of love from watching his parents together made him quite certain that this constant tension was neither necessary nor desirable.

Gretchen had shed tears before letting him out of the car in front of the bus station in Seattle. "Of course, of course, you're right," she'd said one minute, and "damn it, Colin, don't let it go" she'd insisted furiously the next. "You're like crosstown traffic," she'd concluded sadly, as he got out of the car with his backpack and guitar. The tires screeched as Gretchen pulled away from the curb, and as she turned left at the corner she stuck her arm out the window, flipping him off.

6

When the old man with the guitar started to sing, he sang in a voice that was as rough as his hands. His gravelly baritone sent a thrill through the room, and Colin noticed people nodding their heads. Though Colin couldn't understand any of them, each word the man sang had an incantatory power, and seemed to hold a layer of meaning for each year that he had lived. The song seemed to bind the listeners to the singer and to each other. They shared an identity with roots in antiquity, an identity that found its expression in this taut relationship between singer and audience.

Colin realized that this was a sound that couldn't possibly last. When the old man with the guitar died or stopped singing, this would only be a memory left for those few who'd been here on this night, or on any thousand of other such nights. Even if the man had made a recording, there was no perpetual radio play that could reproduce the unique magic of this live performance in this dimly lit bar on this rainy evening, where the timeless shared identity of the listeners provided a foundation of heartbeat rhythm for the magician's voice and strings.

That it would not last, Colin realized, added a sharp poignancy to this sound, which was so much more than sound. It was a sound that would last as long as it could last, to a dying breath, to a final heartbeat, to a last flicker of memory. It would even last in Colin now, though he couldn't understand the words, and was present only as an outsider to be shifted and changed by these vibrations without contributing to them. For a while longer it might endure as the stuff of stories or second-hand memory, but it would eventually be lost altogether, dust to dust.

As he settled with the bartender and shouldered his backpack, Colin remembered Stevie Kassabian's laughter. His ambition was even more preposterous than either of them had supposed. Colin wanted his work to live, but he also wanted it to have the mortality of heartbeat and memory. For him, there was no such dimly lit bar, no small and tight-knit community of speakers of an ancient language. There was no intimate and beleaguered shared identity, and no promise of long-term recollection and gradual fading away. What he wanted was impossible to contrive, but that didn't stop him from yearning, now all the more painfully.

Colin made his solitary way back to the station through streets that were emptier now that night had fallen. The rain came down steadily and the lights from storefronts were reflected on the wet pavement. Six weeks earlier, the mysteriousness of language and culture in the Basque country would have drawn him in irresistibly. Now he boarded his train eagerly, and returned the polite Spanish greetings of his fellow travelers with relief as he settled himself and his belongings in the compartment.

7

The train arrived in Salamanca at two o'clock the next afternoon. Colin paused on the street outside the station to get his bearings. In the course of his travels, he'd learned that he could find his way to the center of most small cities if he just took a moment or two to watch the pedestrians, and to get a sense of the way the streets were laid out.

The street the station was on was lined with narrow sidewalks and post-war buildings. He couldn't put his finger on what it was exactly, but things seemed to be tending toward the left. So, Colin turned left and started walking. Within another block, he saw a sign marked *centro ciudad* with an arrow confirming that he'd made the right choice.

It hadn't taken him more than a few minutes on the streets of Madrid earlier that morning to decide to move on right away in search of a place that would be more Spanish and less of an international capital. He also wanted to find a place where the dominant sounds would not always be the sounds of traffic. He was listening for the remnants of an older world.

Following the flow of pedestrians, and the occasional signs, Colin crossed a broad boulevard in front of a small park and made his way up a narrow street that led him under an archway that opened on the Plaza Mayor. Colin heard footsteps, the tinkling of silverware and cups on saucers, voices and laughter. Tables from bars and restaurants overflowed into the plaza, which was populated with hundreds of people standing, walking, sitting, looking around, or absorbed in each other. The whole was bathed in a golden light that radiated from the stone facades and columns.

A church bell tolled the half hour. A moment later, Colin heard another bell, farther off, and then another and another. A stork with a six-foot wingspan circled the plaza's clock tower, clacking its long beak before settling in an immense nest made of branches that rested precariously on the top of the tower. A flock of sharp-crying swallows rushed the circumference of the plaza in a dizzy swirl, a dark-haired mother pointed them out to her young daughter saying *mira, niña, como giran las golondrinas.*

Colin repeated the phrase to himself, taking pleasure in the shape of the words and in the shapes that his lips and tongue needed to form in order to utter them. Church bells, birds, footsteps, and this soft-edged language everywhere: this was a soundscape that he couldn't hear anywhere at home.

The arched entrances to the plaza were arranged asymmetrically. Three passageways opened into the square plaza immediately beneath the clock tower. On another side of the square, steps led down to a covered marketplace. A corner archway, nearly opposite to where Colin had entered, revealed the Romanesque doorway to a twelfth century church whose walls merged with the walls of the plaza itself.

As had happened in other places during his travels, Colin felt himself drawn toward the shallow stone steps that led up to the wooden doors of the church. After the brightness of the open plaza, it took a moment for his eyes to adjust to the dimly lit interior. Between the coolness of the still air and the damp earthy smell of the stone, Colin felt as if he'd descended into the bowels of the earth. The church was empty. The silence and calm, so few steps from the bustle of the open plaza, were absolute.

When the bells tolled three o'clock, the sound seemed to come from another world. Colin passed through the wooden doors again, and was immediately returned to the commotion of the city's center. Back into the plaza, and then out again through another arch, Colin flowed as if on the surface of a stream pulled in complex patterns by gravity.

His steps led him along a stone street overshadowed by high stone walls that opened up onto another open space. Rectangular, with a garden and grassy area in the center, a sign on the wall identified it as the Plaza de la Libertad. There was no commotion here. Just café tables along one wall, the quiet of the surrounding buildings, and a view back through the archway into the Plaza Mayor.

Colin propped his backpack and guitar against the stone wall, and took a seat at one of the café tables. He'd need to find a place to stay and to leave his things, and then he'd need to go out and find the music. He ordered a beer.

Two tables away, a young woman sat alone. She was the only other customer.

As Colin sipped his beer, he thought about the lyrics that he'd been working on, and the sound that he hadn't yet found for them. He watched the passing pedestrians, and enjoyed picking up scraps of their conversations. He took pleasure in the warm glow of reflected sunlight on the tops of the buildings. But his eyes kept returning to the young woman at the nearby table.

She was writing and sketching in a notebook. Now and then, she paused thoughtfully with the end of her pen in her mouth. Her eyes sought the top of the building opposite, as if she were trying to describe the pattern that had been carved into the stone there.

She was beautiful. Colin only caught the radiance of her smile at second hand. But he realized that, like the dove he'd seen on the street in Irún, the sight that he'd had of this woman, with her postcards, her notebook, and her smile, would be one of the images that he would carry away with him, to define forever the memory of his arrival in Spain. Though she didn't seem to be in any hurry to leave, Colin was suddenly filled with terrible anxiety that she'd get up to go, and that he'd be left to drink his cold beer alone in the Plaza de la Libertad.

1

After three weeks in Spain, Juliet had grown more accustomed to men's stares than she'd ever imagined possible. Spanish men were brazen in a way that most American men had stopped being decades ago. She'd lost track of the number of times that conversations stopped completely as she passed by men gathered outside a bar. They stopped and stared, and remarked audibly on aspects of her appearance.

Somehow they always knew that she was a foreigner. *Americana,* they'd say, trying to get her to look. Or *inglesa.* Once she heard *sueca,* when a group of middle aged men mistook her for a Swede for some reason, though it took her a few blocks to realize what they'd said. From the comments of Spanish men, she knew that she had hips and legs, a chest, and a head of blonde hair that were objects of some admiration.

She'd never really broken herself down quite so anatomically before, and in a bemused way had almost grown halfway grateful for the new level of self-awareness. Spanish women she'd spoken to took some satisfaction from being at the receiving end of this kind of street analysis. *Piropos* was the word they used for these remarks from men who were strangers.

Juliet saw right away that this young man's stare was different. As she returned her eyes to her notebook, she thought about how curious a thing it was that there could be a perceptibly different quality about the way someone looked at you. She rested the end of her pen on her lower lip and tried to puzzle it out. The eyes were fixed in the same way, making the object of their focus totally unmistakable.

No. Most of the stares she'd been subjected to had slithered down the length of her body and then back up again to her eyes. The message was clear: the onlooker found her desirable as an object of consumption, and wanted her to know it. But this young man's eyes had met her own and they'd remained there, expressing an interest in who she was, not just in how she looked. And then, he'd turned away entirely, as if an architectural detail on the far side of the plaza had suddenly demanded his attention.

Juliet had finished her *café con leche*. She shook her head politely when the waiter asked her if she wanted anything else. She had made a schedule for herself, and rarely had to think twice about sticking to it. Then she felt the young man looking at her again, and she found herself thinking that maybe she should have asked for a second cup of coffee. She knew that the picturesque little plaza would only grow more beautiful as the rays of the afternoon sun grew longer, and knew that she was the only one holding herself accountable for how she spent her time.

She'd stopped for coffee at this café on the afternoon of her first day in the city, and she had returned to sit there and read or write for an hour almost every day since. It was, she'd decided, her favorite spot in Salamanca.

But today, it wasn't the quiet allure of the gem-like Plaza de la Libertad that made her reluctant to give up her table. After a moment's struggle, Juliet had to admit to herself that it was the look in those deep blue eyes that was making it hard for her to leave.

That acknowledgement was all it took for her to make up her mind to go. She had no time for nonsense. She put her pen and notebook in her purse.

"*Si te quedas, te compro un café.*" *If you stay, I'll buy you a coffee.* Colin had been summoning up his courage, and rehearsing the invitation ever since she'd waved away the waiter.

Juliet looked up sharply at the sound of his voice. The Spanish was unexpected. From the backpack and the guitar, she'd assumed he was a foreigner, like her.

"*¿Me estás hablando a mí?*" *Are you talking to me?* Even as the words left her lips, she felt like an idiot. Of course he was speaking to her. They were the only two customers, and the waiter had gone inside. But the Spanish had caught her off guard. *It must be this rhapsody or none*, she thought. Lines from Wallace Stevens' poem about the man with the guitar swam up in her memory, unbidden. *The rhapsody of things as they are.*

"*Si tomas un café conmigo, a lo mejor me podrás contar algo de la ciudad. Acabo de llegar a Salamanca, y nunca he estado aquí.*" *If you have a cup of coffee with me, maybe you could tell me a little about the city. I just arrived in Salamanca, and I've never been here before.*

This time Juliet could tell from his cadence and intonation that Spanish was not his language. He spoke it well, but it was formal and a bit rigid. The word *theatrical* came to mind, but even as she wondered whether he'd rehearsed what he was going to say before speaking, she was smiling back at him.

"So, you're going to buy me a cup of coffee?" she said, closing her purse decidedly and pushing her chair back. "No. Don't get up. I'll join you over there, so you don't have to move your whole kit and caboodle."

"Kit and caboodle!" He laughed warmly, and Juliet felt her chest and neck flush with something that was not exactly embarrassment. "I guess you must speak English, then," he said, and Juliet had to laugh, too.

Colin had gotten up, despite her protest. He pulled another chair alongside his own so that they could sit side by side with their backs to the golden stone and share the view of the plaza. He didn't sit down again until she had. It was the sort of gentlemanly gesture that her mother would have noticed and appreciated, and it made him seem older than he looked.

2

Conversation came easily to them. Too easily, Juliet thought at first, unsettled by her spontaneity. It made her uneasy to feel so comfortable and so relaxed by the side of this very good-looking young man. She was engaged to be married, she kept telling herself. And: there was nothing wrong with talking with someone.

With that, maybe she'd convinced herself. What was certain was that she wasn't thinking about it at all by the time the waiter brought her the promised cup of coffee. As the golden stone on the opposite side of the plaza glowed ever more warmly in the lengthening rays of the afternoon sun, Juliet felt herself glowing, too. As she hadn't felt herself glowing since…well, she couldn't remember if she'd ever felt quite this way. It was as if, after nearly four carefully structured weeks there, she'd finally woken up to the fact that she was on the other side of the world from home, in lovely, legendary Salamanca.

Home dropped away completely for her before she'd finished that second cup of coffee. She'd held home close to her until then, with her solitary routine of classes, and postcards, and the sightseeing walks around town that she plotted out ahead of time on the map of the city that she'd bought the day she'd arrived. All told, she had four weeks and two days to spend in Spain and from the very first day she'd intended to make the most of every minute. But her awareness of the shortness of time meant that she hadn't really left home behind.

Home was the brief remainder of the summer, which she would spend with her parents and hanging out by the pool with her sister Jackie, before heading off to Cornell to start her graduate studies in systematic botany. And home also meant Brad, her fiancé. He was at work, so they couldn't see much of each other during the week. But they could have their Friday night dinners out, and their Saturdays and Sundays together. And throughout the week, they could begin every morning with a quick phone call and end every night with a longer one, just as they had since she was a sophomore in college.

Juliet had called Brad collect when she'd first arrived in Spain, and on each Saturday after that. They'd both agreed that it was too expensive to talk more often, and Juliet had made up the difference at first by mailing him a postcard every other day, and by trying to keep a regular diary that she'd be able to share with him when she returned. "So that it will feel like you've been there with me, and seen all that I'll have seen."

Even as she got up from her table to join Colin for that second cup of coffee, Juliet thought about how she'd describe it in her diary entry for the day. *A handsome young man with long-ish hair and the bluest eyes I've ever seen asked me to join him for a cup of coffee, and for some reason I just couldn't refuse.* Obviously, for Brad's eyes, that wouldn't do at all. But it was the truth, and Juliet was a stickler for telling the truth, especially in her diary.

The Plaza de la Libertad, cloister-like, was silent save for the sharp cries of circling *golondrinas*, the flamenco clatter of passing heels on stone, and the distant tumult of the lively crowd that populated the Plaza Mayor at the end of the street, beyond the great archway. This was all part of the truth, too, Juliet thought.

Whatever she wrote in her diary, whatever Brad read, he wouldn't be able to feel the enchantment of the place as she did. Brad, for all of his attractive warmth and charm, was not susceptible to enchantment of place. This was a truth that she'd noticed during the first summer they'd spent together, when evening would find them on the dock at her grandmother's lake house surrounded by a magic of fireflies and purple sky and quiet splashes in the black water. Brad cast and reeled in his line, seemingly enjoying the little nibbles as much as bringing in a fish. Juliet just sat with her feet dangling in the August-warm lake, hardly able to breathe lest the magic snatch itself away and leave her awkward in her bikini and only nineteen and the skin on her lower legs turning to goose-pimples.

Brad, fishing purposefully beside her, never felt the moment as she did. He never seemed entirely able to see and feel what she saw and felt, even when she grabbed his arm and tried to point something out to him. He laughed once, when she talked of the faerie hour, and then he took her by the hand and led her up the path toward the houselights to deliver his string of freshly caught fish to her mother and grandmother in the kitchen. A truth that Brad never knew was that, even as she followed him inside, so happy to have her hand in his, Juliet left a part of herself outside, caught up in the faerie hour, on the lakeshore, in the purple night.

And now it was truth that Juliet felt like she knew this place intimately, though she'd only been there for less than a month. Keeping track of the details in her diary and postcards may have sharpened her senses, but words fell short.

Of their climate, the *salmantinos* liked to say *nueve meses de invierno y tres de infierno*. In the midst of this infernal summer, Juliet had found heaven--in the red Sahara dust that filled the sky at sunset and painted parked cars with a coating of Africa, in the intoxicating smell of damp earth and grassland that rushed through the city before a thundershower, and in the musical clamor of bleating and bells that drew her to her window in the middle of the night to see enormous flocks of sheep being driven right through the city streets.

She wouldn't be ready to leave Salamanca, and when she did leave a part of her would remain behind. She knew. She'd begun to feel it tearing away already with less than a week left of her visit. Despite all of her thoughtful planning, time was just going to have its terrible way with her, leaving her grasping and unsatisfied. She resented it.

"*Y ahora, ¿qué?*" Colin said, trying out his Spanish again, and enjoying the percussive sensation of the tip of his tongue against the roof of his mouth as he pronounced his "r" as correctly as could be desired. *Now what?*

Juliet had finished her cup of coffee. All that was left of Colin's *caña* was the rim of foam that the cold *Mahou* had left around the inside of the glass.

"*Ahora, tomamos otro,*" Juliet said decisively, as the bells of the city began to peal the hour in clamorous confirmation. "*¿No crees?*" *Now we have another. Don't you think?*

3

Sitting beside Juliet in the warmth of the afternoon, Colin felt the dropping away, too. It wasn't home that dropped away for him, but instead the restless anxiety about his work that had driven him across the Atlantic and then halfway across Europe. He'd been so caught up in searching for the ineffable something that he hoped would resolve his misgivings about his music and lyrics that he hadn't been able to be fully present to his surroundings.

For the most part, they looked out toward the plaza while they spoke. He watched the gentle, unconscious, movements of Juliet's hands as she told him about her studies, the flora of Castilla, and about the hidden shrines to the Virgin that she'd discovered here and there during her explorations of the city.

Juliet had sharp eyes and her attention had been drawn to things that Colin would never have noticed on his own. While he surveyed landscapes and cityscapes for striking sounds, Juliet saw complex relationships of light and shadow and life of all kinds. Flowers in window boxes, trees protected by iron lattice-work, gardens hidden behind high stone walls inhabited by wide-eyed cats. She'd exchanged early morning smiles with rumpled middle-aged women in bedroom slippers holding watering cans, pausing in a shaft of sunlight. It was an unspoken bond she'd discovered to be a constant on both sides of the Atlantic. Some, like her, lived lives entwined with the organic world of plants, persisting through the seasons amidst the bustle and crush of the human world.

She strongly believed in that persistence, and in a modern human world that could coexist with, and be much improved by, the eternal presence of simpler, more durable life. The famous stones of Salamanca did not fascinate her as much as the greenery which lasted in its cracks and in-between places.

She talked, and made him talk with her questions. They were questions that struck him as wild and out of the blue. What did his dreams sound like? Did he sing as he played the guitar, or did he play the guitar as he sang? Did he know that in Andalucía during Holy Week men took turns singing compliments to the Virgin Mary as she was carried past?

Now and then, he turned in his chair so that he could see her face, trying to make the movement seem a natural one. Trying not to be too obvious about simply wanting to look at her. Each time he did, he had to turn away again quickly. Her eyes shined and flashed with life as she spoke. He found himself admiring the geometry of that triangle below her ear where neck turned to cheek. There seemed to be a layer of warm light spread beneath her skin. She was so real that it made his head swim.

It was easier to watch her hands on the edge of the table. Her fingers were slender, her nails were nicely kept but unpainted. They lifted and danced with excitement to punctuate her description of Mérida, the old Roman city far to the south, in Extremadura. She'd spent seven hours on a bus to get there during her first week in Spain. The stones of the ancient wall there, she said, were the size of Volkswagens. No mortar held them in place. Two thousand years of civilization, if you could call it that. As Santa Eulalia was martyred, a dove had flown out of her mouth. Juliet had spent an hour walking around in the dried grass that grew untamed around the base of the aqueduct, brushing the old stones with her fingertips, marveling at the brickwork (so familiar it had seemed to her!), and wondering at time.

Colin noticed the ring on her finger, of course. He wondered about that, and about the man who'd been able both to claim her and to let her go so far away without him. But though the diamond flashed with her gestures, Juliet said nothing about it, and Colin didn't ask.

Juliet was telling him about the shriveled fig of a thing that she'd seen in a reliquary in Alba de Tormes, and that was said to be the heart of Santa Teresa, when the waiter approached their table to ask if he could bring them something more. The waiter was an elderly gentleman with a fringe of gray hair above his ears and a stomach that betrayed a weakness for food and drink. The shirt he wore was crisply pressed and immaculately white, and Colin could see from the way he smiled at them both that he was pleased that they'd stayed so long at his café.

"I've got nowhere to go," Colin said, with a shrug. *And nowhere I'd rather be*. After all his travels, the sound that he'd found and now wanted to go on hearing, was that of this young American woman's captivating voice, speaking to him about age-old mysteries in his own native language. From this kind of magic something wonderful begged to be born.

4

The heart of the saint, if that's what it truly was, looked as dry as dust. Juliet remembered thinking that if it hadn't been safely sealed behind glass, it would crumble away to nothing in the least breath of wind. And then she'd spent the rest of the morning touring the old stones of Alba de Tormes musing about all that separated our first dust from our last.

The saint had once been as alive as Juliet was now. Teresa's sandaled feet grew dusty with the very same earth that now got between Juliet's toes. She had inhaled the aroma of this same countryside, and felt the same summer sun on her shoulders. Santa Teresa had thought of herself, her most secret self, as living deep within an interior castle. Seven walls, and seven sheltered rooms, each one farther inside and more perfect than the last. Only one knew the way through them all, and held the key and could pass between them to arrive at the innermost chamber, and that one was not even herself, not without years of struggle and surrender.

Juliet had come to the same café every afternoon, as if she'd somehow known that this was where Colin Hogan would choose to stop for a cold beer when he arrived in Salamanca. It was crazy to think that way, she knew. But it was crazy, too, that the name of the Plaza de la Libertad hadn't meant anything in particular to her until she smiled back at the gentlemanly old waiter and said "*¿porqué no?*" *Why not?*

The truth inside her was her own to unlock. She'd known for years that Brad couldn't make his way through to the sheltered room, not even all that far inside of her, where all it took was a shift in light, and the open question in a pair of ocean blue eyes, for Juliet to find herself living in a world of magic.

"*Dust to dust* might be accurate in some loose way," she protested, as the waiter returned with their drinks. But it was far from fair to pack all of this, all that took place in between the first dust and the last, into that tiny little two-letter preposition and just run right past it as if it were nothing.

She'd tried to record her thoughts about this in her diary the day she'd gone to Alba de Tormes, but had given up and scratched out the half-formed paragraph. The words came so much more easily to her now, as she shared her train of thought about the sixteenth-century saint and an overlooked preposition, with this young American man who'd sat down beside her.

"All of this." Juliet sketched a gesture with her hand that was meant to encompass the metal chairs and tables of the café, the narrow street that led away in the distance to the more heavily trafficked streets of the city, the billowy white cloud in the blue sky above them, the plains of Castilla rolling and heaving their way down south to the Sierra de Gredos.

"That's some pretty special dust," Colin agreed.

Juliet was grateful that they were sitting side by side, because it felt good to be gushing with such unrestricted enthusiasm. She didn't think it would come so easily if she were facing him, with those eyes watching her too closely.

As she knelt in her Prairie Village garden, with the afternoon sun on her shoulders and a fistful of rich soil in each hand, Juliet remembered the look in those eyes when he'd agreed with her about the special dust. She remembered realizing that he knew about it already, that he'd given it plenty of thought before she ever said anything. No one she'd ever met had been so acutely aware of how densely packed that little preposition was between the two dusts.

Colin Hogan vibrated with life. She remembered how alive he'd felt beside her, how it had felt like waking up, or like doors swinging open. She remembered the brush of his forearm against hers, like an electric charge.

She remembered that afternoon in the Plaza de la Libertad so vividly. When she closed her eyes, damp with gratitude, some of the details were as plain as the sight of her garden fence when she blinked them open again. His hat resting on an empty chair. The comfortable-looking leather boots he wore. His white guitar. She'd reviewed every detail, words and appearances, again and again until they had merged into the single story that was hers alone to tell. And yet, there was still so much lost.

She had been furious with herself for not describing more of it in her diary. *If only*, she had thought more times than she could count. She had driven herself mad with impossible bargains and alternate realities. She would have liked…she would have loved…to live through that afternoon again. To be able to grasp and hold onto every passing fleck of conversation, to be able to trace the invisible threads as they wove their way between them.

PART
THREE

1

Colin's plan for Salamanca, as it had been for his travels in France, Ireland, and England, was to find a likely bar or two in town where he'd be allowed to perform for tips. Living on the cheap, he'd been able to make his savings stretch a long way.

"I've come across a few bars that might do the trick," Juliet said. "I could show you where they are, if you like. Maybe save you some time." She made the offer before she was altogether aware of what she was doing. It came naturally enough.

"Well, I thank you kindly, ma'am," Colin said, with a smile. "That's right friendly of you."

Before they left, Colin asked if he could leave his things at the bar until he'd found a place to say. The waiter was happy to oblige, and Colin and Juliet left the Plaza de la Libertad together as the afternoon turned to evening.

With the cooler air, the native *salmantinos* began to populate the Plaza Mayor in force. Young, middle-aged, and old, they circled the plaza in chattering crowds or flocks like earthbound swallows. Meeting old friends and new, they interrupted their circling with stops for *pinchos*. Every bar had specialty items, and Colin caught tantalizing glimpses of small plates being handed around with tiny glasses of *vino tinto*: *aceitunas, pimientos de piquillo, salpicón, mejillones en escabeche, jeta, salchichón, jamón serrano, queso manchego*.

Juliet supplied the words for things that he didn't recognize. Colin repeated them back to her, savoring the consonants in his throat and with his tongue and lips as if he were tasting the foods themselves. He made faces as he pronounced, exaggerating her own, and they both laughed. They didn't eat or drink anywhere, they just walked slowly around the Plaza with the crowd, stopping to peer in windows now and then to get a closer look at the offerings inside. Juliet felt bolder, freer to move about and to stop and stare. Having a companion, and having dropped out of her routine for the day, felt liberating.

The sky above the Plaza turned from purple to black, and floodlights extended the golden glow of the ancient stone into the night. The crowds grew noisier, larger, and younger, as the older people and families began to retire and Castilla's youth took to the streets for their night-long *marcha*.

Juliet had been out late a few times early in her stay, following along with a crowd of her fellow students as they drank and danced their way from *Camelot* to *Morgana* to *El Submarino*—clubs in fantastic architectural settings that throbbed with music and writhing bodies until moments before dawn. She'd returned home each time with a headache and sore feet, to sleep half the day away and wake up in the early afternoon, groggy and disoriented.

The night life of Salamanca, she'd quickly decided, was not for her. She felt no appetite for the dueling glances, or for the charges of magnetic attraction that so obviously kept her companions wired and alive through the night no matter how much they'd had to drink. She'd passed on subsequent invitations to *salir de marcha* in favor of returning early to her apartment to memorize vocabulary and study verb forms, sometimes after going to the movies with Greta and Magda, the pair of eighty-three year old twin sisters from New York who were spending their third consecutive summer studying Spanish together in Salamanca.

ROMEO'S BE*A*T

But now, Juliet felt the energy of the night pulsing with gentle insistence in her own veins. A part of her felt like dancing.

She wanted to grab this stranger's hand and feel whether his palms, too, felt damp in the warm night. She wanted to feel him swing and pull her around in a crowd of bodies in motion. She wanted to feel like she was flying, lifted up and bouncing on a current of music.

All of this was another truth that would be hard to account for in the diary that she'd started out keeping for Brad's eyes. She lightly shrugged away the nagging feeling that her decisions and actions were out of synch.

"Come on," she said. "I promised I'd show you some bars where you might be able to play."

"Lead away," Colin said, holding out his hand.

Juliet reached out and took it. His hand was as warm as her own. His fingers closed around hers and held on as she pulled him across the main current of pedestrians and under one of the archways that led out of the Plaza. When they reached the quiet corner by the steps of the old church, she opened her hand slightly, and he let go.

"San Martín," Colin said, gesturing at the frieze above the church door that showed the saint on horseback. "I was in there for a few minutes earlier today. Massive columns, dark and dank. My kind of a place."

"It's my favorite church in the city."

"Funny kind of a saint, right? There Saint Francis goes, heading out into the streets naked, and all Saint Martin can spare for the poor beggar on the side of the road is *half* of his cloak?"

"Do you want to hear my theory?"

"Please!"

"I'd always wondered about that half gesture, too." Juliet began, a bit shyly. But seeing that his interest was real, she went on boldly. "I came by here one afternoon a couple of weeks ago, after having spent too long walking around out in the sun. I went inside, just to sit down for a minute. I put down my shopping bags. It was so quiet and so cool. I wasn't the only one. There were a couple of other women, and they had their shopping bags with them, too. I felt like we were sisters.

41

That's when I understood St. Martin for the first time. He's the perfect saint for ordinary people like me. Not everybody is going to be like St. Francis, and go all the way, give it all up, and take to the streets naked with a begging bowl in hand. Some of us, maybe even most of us, are going to want to hang on to something. We may be willing enough to give, but it will only be a partial gift, like St. Martin with his half cloak.

"And what good is half a cloak, right? I mean, it's ruined. It's not whole anymore. But the sainthood of St. Martin is about grace, you see? Even a partial gift, even half a cloak, is enough for sainthood, because grace makes up the difference. It's more accessible for ordinary people than the extremism of St. Francis."

"And so they put his church in exactly the right spot."

"Yes! Right here in the heart of the city. It's built right into the wall of the Plaza so that ordinary commercial life and sanctuary in God's peace are conjoined."

"Conjoined."

Juliet felt herself flush. "It's a bit much, isn't it?"

"Well…it's a bit more theological than I bargained for. I thought we were just going bar hopping."

Still laughing, and somehow holding each other's hands again, they stopped at Aretino, a few steps away from San Martín. They ordered little glasses of red wine and a plate of tiny fried fish. They stood at the bar, facing each other. The place was crowded with people of all ages, and loud with laughter and competing voices.

Colin ate one of the little fish and nodded appreciatively. He sipped his wine and held the little glass in a hand that was strong and lean and tanned. He'd looked around as they came in, with eyes that didn't seem to miss anything. But Juliet felt that his attention was wholly on her.

They stood together in a little English-speaking bubble. Juliet watched his lips move as he spoke. She noted the whiteness of his straight teeth, the little crinkle at the corner of his eyes when he smiled. He smiled at her often, and it felt like warmth inside her.

When the curly-haired woman behind the bar handed them their drinks, Juliet saw her glance at the engagement ring on her finger before shifting her eyes to Colin. Naturally enough, she took him to be her young man, her fiancé, her *novio*. Juliet wondered, with some discomfort, if Colin realized the misunderstanding that they might be creating in anyone who looked at them. If he did, he gave no sign of it.

As she stood there with him, feeling a bit guilty and deceptive, and a little giddy, too, she almost slipped the ring off her finger. But she didn't want to lose it, or to make too obvious a gesture. She thought to herself, "what kind of a girl am I?" But, to her surprise, she felt more inclined to laugh than to disapprove. "I know what kind of a girl I am. I'm the kind of girl who enjoys feeling just like this, who doesn't see anything wrong with it. Who sees everything *right* with it."

Just like this: alive and thousands of miles away from obligations and promises, standing in the electric presence of something greater than herself. Awake and feeling like there's something that matters, or that's at least memorable, in the moment.

Filled with the spirit of the place, Juliet understood the young Spanish women she'd been observing so carefully for weeks. She placed her empty wine glass on the bar, grabbed her young man's forearm with her hand, and said "*venga*." *Come on.* The evening was young. Her time was short.

Brad was thousands of miles away, and whatever she decided to do about him, he would never need to know about the few hours she'd spent wandering the streets of Salamanca in the company of the handsome young man with the deep blue eyes. This was a truth that Juliet decided she could keep for herself.

She made the decision consciously and felt liberated from her own scrupulousness. Brad wasn't keeping a tell-all journal of his every movement for her while she was away, after all. Not that she thought he was going out with any other women, or anything like that. But she wasn't "going out" either. She was just showing someone around town. Someone she'd never see again.

The fact that she found him attractive…well, that was her own private business, a truth that she couldn't do anything about, even if she made a big show of denying it. She shook her head free of the preoccupation and let immediacy and distance do their work together.

Out in the street, Juliet again felt that surge of understanding rush through her like an exotic cocktail. For weeks, she'd experienced Salamanca at night only as an observer, an outsider. Music spilling from the open doorways of crowded bars, the sound of laughter echoing off the canyon-like walls of the narrow streets, the clatter and rhythm of shoes on cobblestones. The night had a pulse to it. Juliet felt it beating.

From Aretino, the Catedral Nueva seemed only steps away at the end of the Rúa Mayor. Floodlights made the immense edifice glow against the backdrop of the night sky. It was a golden mountain of stone. Juliet showed Colin the astronaut that had been recently carved into the cathedral's façade, and with the same sense of local pride, and pride in her own familiarity with the city, walked with him along the *calle de los tres coños*, and told him the story behind the passage's unofficial name. She felt her voice and gestures become distinctly Spanish--*¡Coño! ¡La catedral!* Colin's laughter echoed from the high stone on all sides, encompassing her and carrying her along as their steps led them into the oldest section of the city, along streets too narrow for vehicle traffic.

La Formentera was a tiny little bar, tucked into the wall of a street that sloped steeply down toward the Río Tormes. Tonight there was a bearded man with a guitar. A small space had been kept clear in front of his chair, but the bar was otherwise packed to the rafters. No tourists here…all the patrons were Spanish, and well-dressed. Expensive jewelry sparkled on the necks and hands and ears of the women as they nodded and gestured in time with the serious gaiety of their conversations.

There was space for the two of them only at the bar. They had to stand closely together. Juliet inhaled the warmth of Colin's skin, and felt the warmth rising to her cheeks. She wondered if her eyes glowed and flashed like the eyes of the other women in the bar.

"*Dos botellines de Mahou*," she told the man. And then to Colin she said, "We're lucky. I think we've come on a good night."

"What do you mean?"

"Just wait." She handed him one of the two small icy bottles of beer that the *camarero* placed in front of them.

The man with the guitar began to play, and the room fell silent. Many of the patrons clapped in a complicated rhythm that accented the flourishes of the guitar, while the rest simply watched and listened with rapt attention. And then, three slender raven-haired beauties stepped into the clear space and began to twine around each other, dancing with their graceful hands flowering into living sculptures in the smoky blue air above their heads. This was one of the best moments of her time in Spain, and Juliet's appreciation of it was magnified by the look on Colin's face.

She wondered what sort of a musician he was and wanted to believe that he was a very good one. She was suddenly desperate to hear him play. Did he sing, too? His speaking voice was lovely.

Colin's eyes followed the dancers' hands. He stood straight and tall, his body taut with attention, his chest not much more than six inches away from her own. Juliet couldn't take her eyes away from him, and she was intensely grateful that his attention was elsewhere.

She would never be entirely sure how long they stood there like that together. At some point, she asked the *camarero* for a second round of beers. One piece was succeeded by the next, interrupted only by the applause and cheers of the patrons. The atmosphere was intense, but muted, as if they were all involved in some clandestine activity that could not be allowed to reach far into the street outside.

At some point, the guitarist suddenly put his instrument aside. "*¡Dame algo frío, por Dios!*" he shouted, clutching at his throat dramatically. Someone passed him a cold beer, and the crowd relaxed. In silent accord, Juliet and Colin made their way to the door and out into the cooler air.

The street was sparsely lit, with only a single lamp fixed to the wall of a building on the corner. The light spilling from the doorway and small window of the bar they'd just left painted the uneven cobblestones in sharp relief. Colin stepped ahead of her into the darkness and paused there with his head tipped backwards. Juliet followed his gaze upwards. The narrow street of dark sky between the tops of the buildings was spangled with bright stars.

"Wow." The sound he uttered was mostly an exhalation.

"Amazing, isn't it?"

"Same old streets. Same old sky. This old, old world."

"It's not the same at home, is it? Just because the buildings aren't as old, or the streets aren't as narrow…"

"Or because of all the light pollution, maybe? I noticed it when I was in Carcassonne a few weeks ago. You can really see how much drier the air is here, though. There's the Milky Way!"

"*La via lactea*. The Camino de Santiago. The pilgrims used to follow it from all over Europe on their way to the shrine in Galicia. They still do."

"Have you been?"

"Not yet. I was hoping to get there, but I fly home in at the end of the week so I guess it's going to have to wait for the next trip."

Something inside her snapped, as though she'd broken a rule in a game she'd never played before. She looked at him for reassurance. His smile was uncertain.

Their steps led them downhill toward the Tormes. Music, laughter, and the sound of glassware emerged from bars along the banks, but the sounds did not cut far into the stillness of the night. They turned away from the sound and followed the city walls, and went out and stood in the center of the Puente Romano, beside the headless stone bull on its pedestal. Juliet had never ventured here after dark. With Colin beside her, she felt again that surge of bravery, that freedom that allowed her to go places that she couldn't go alone.

The sky above the bridge widened out, so that they could see stars twinkling among the branches of the trees along the river's bank. The old city rose up behind them, a mountain of glowing stone crowned by the tower and dome of the Catedral Nueva. For a while they stood there listening to the slow, sad trickle of the weary Tormes, and then they climbed up again into the livelier sounds of the city at night.

Remembering that Colin's plan was to find a bar or two where he might be able to play, Juliet led him past some of the places that she thought might be suitable. They both lost track of time. The hour was late when they found themselves where they'd begun, in the Plaza de la Libertad.

Colin didn't recognize the place right away, now floodlit and with café tables and chairs already stacked neatly. "I better get my stuff before he locks up for the night."

"And I guess I better get home to bed. I've got class early tomorrow."

"If you wait a sec, I'll walk you to your door."

"Okay. But you really already have."

Colin glanced back at her, but was already stepping into the bar to thank the white-haired *camarero* for minding his things. He emerged a minute later, with his pack on his back and his guitar in his hand.

Juliet pointed at a doorway on the opposite side of the plaza.

"See! I live right over there."

He walked with her anyway. Juliet was sleepy and her feet were tired, and she dimly wondered how tired he must be feeling. It had probably been something like fourteen or fifteen hours since he'd stepped off the train.

He thanked her for having welcomed him so warmly, and they said vague things to each other about enjoying their remaining travels. They exchanged *dos besos*, Spanish-style, pressing their cheeks together briefly on either side. Colin waited until the glass entryway door locked her safely inside. Juliet waved, and watched as he turned and walked away across the plaza. The entryway light went off--it was on a timer. She continued to stand there at the door, looking out at the empty plaza.

Upstairs, in the comfortable little room that had felt homey and snug to her from the first moment she'd seen it, Juliet undressed for bed. She was very tired, and as she unbuttoned her blouse she watched her fingers with a peculiar feeling of disembodiment.

Her engagement ring sparkled in the light cast by the too-bright lamp on the ceiling. When Brad, down on one knee, had shown it to her in its little blue box she had loved it immediately. They had never talked about rings, but it was exactly what she would have picked for herself. It was all the more perfect because Brad had done it on his own. She'd said yes to his question without hesitation. What she'd wanted was a secure place to plant her heart…so that love could have all its mighty fertile way with her, lift her high up with intricate canopy into her biggest, bravest life.

She stepped out of her skirt and hung it neatly in the doorless alcove that served as a closet. She'd worn sandals all day, and her feet were dusty from the streets of the city. Normally, she just washed them off in the sink before getting into bed, but not tonight. She removed her ring before getting in the shower, as she always did, and stood in the tiny stall for a long time, letting the warm water run, first down her back, and then on her face and chest.

She toweled herself off lightly, leaving her skin still damp to cool her in the warm night air. She pulled a loosely fitting cotton nightgown over her head, shut the light off, and climbed into her single bed. Tired as she was, something was awake in her that had been dormant for a long time. The nighttime beat of the city had finally gotten under her skin. She understood, now, the urge to be out there with it. He had stood so close to her when they were in the crowded bar. She inhaled the warm smell of his skin and shivered deliciously, touched her chest where he'd pressed his own against her.

Later, she opened her eyes and saw that dawn had changed the sky outside her small window to light purple. She thought of Brad then, and of how very far behind her he seemed. How very far away from her he seemed even when she was with him. That her heart might have outgrown this pot was not a new thought, and the recurrence of it made her shift uncomfortably. She pushed her pillow into an odd shape, and nestled the side of her face into it.

Then, with a surge of anxiety that rinsed through her from head to toe, she realized that she had no idea where Colin was staying or how long he would be in Salamanca. He had turned and walked away, and it hadn't occurred to her to ask.

"Never mind," she told herself, shoving at her pillow again. In a very few days, she was going to be on her way.

The small room brightened with the advance of the morning. Juliet slept fitfully, her usual regimen all awry on account of the late night.

2

Colin loved waking up in a new town. The sun was already bright outside his shuttered window when he opened his eyes to the sound of church bells. He counted three different sources of the sound. Three different distances, in three different directions. None of the bells was perfectly musical. Each was a bit more of a clang than a chime. They were all out of time with one another and yet, together, it worked perfectly, as it did in all of the towns that he'd visited during his travels.

The regular sound of these bells was missing from the soundscapes of the American cities that he knew. With his head still on the pillow, he imagined again how differently attuned one must be--not just to metallic tones and to the musical possibilities of disharmony, but to the passage and meaning of time--growing up in a world of church bells.

He sat up to reach for his guitar, and made the attempt again. Bells are percussive, and so was Colin's guitar. For a few minutes after the bells had stopped, he carried on doing his best to capture their tones and rhythms with the bright atonal splash of fingers on strings. Even when he was satisfied with the discrete package of sound, situating it within a larger compositional context remained something that he needed to figure out.

He pulled his notebook and pen out of his pack, and moved the room's single wooden chair close to the window. He raised the shade and swung both panes wide, flooding the small room with light and air. The street below was busy with people, and Colin itched to get out there into it.

But first there were a few lines he had to get down. His head still filled with the music he'd heard at La Formentera, the sounds came to him in Spanish. The long, drawn-out vowels, a dozen notes or more of raspy eloquence that came straight from the gut. He didn't want to be writing in Spanish. He just wanted to capture some of that rasp and gut and match it to the familiar shape of the American love song.

He'd met another man's woman and he'd never be the same. She'd stood so close to him that he could smell the perfume of her skin. A stranger saw the ring on her finger and thought she was with him. With him, but not with him. Such a pretty ring. His diamond cut us clean apart. Nothing harder than that diamond, clear and sharp, the light goes through and breaks my heart.

It wasn't amounting to much, but he played with it for awhile, filling a page with disjointed words and phrases. Singing a bit in a low voice, trying to draw out his vowels. Lyrical work was Colin's morning practice, wherever he went. And though he'd been vague about the timeframe and had been traveling at a pace that was far from hectic, Stevie Kassabian's exasperation was never far from his mind. He kept the pressure on himself, knowing that the sooner he felt finished and got himself back to the studio in LA, the better.

The five c's? Or was it four? Clarity, and cut, and carat. Colin scratched his head, trying to remember what his aunt had once told him about the yellow diamond his Uncle Edward had bought her for their tenth anniversary. He couldn't think of the other c's, but decided that clarity and cut were all that the lyric would bear without sounding like some kind of jingle.

He got lost in it for awhile. The sensation of intense attraction and immediate loss was rich with potential for song. Her name was Juliet, and she was so beautiful that all of Salamanca was nothing but a backdrop for the time he'd spent with her. It could have all dropped away and been replaced by a flat space and a line of telephone poles and he'd have hardly noticed the difference. But that diamond on her finger made things clear, cut things off.

Through this morning practice, trying to get the essence of this down in words that would hold together in patterns that would evoke the sequential feelings of gain and loss, Colin managed to sort himself out quite happily. He could have spent the better part of the day at it. But from his perch in the window he could count four bell towers topped with the most enormous birds' nests he'd ever seen.

Maybe he would stay indoors all day on his third or fourth day in Salamanca, but not on the first. The call to explore the outside was stronger than the call to plumb the depths any more deeply. The *pensión* was inexpensive, at just over twenty dollars for the night, and so Colin was neither surprised nor very disappointed to discover that the water in the tiny shower stall reached only a lukewarm temperature and ran in four thin streams. It was enough. He patiently washed his long hair and shaved. He found a clean shirt in his pack. He'd rolled it to minimize the wrinkling, a trick his sister had taught him on the eve of his departure.

After the death of his parents, Colin had been so caught up in looking after his sister that he never really paused to feel the effect of the loss. Once he'd been traveling around on his own for a while, however, he had begun to notice little things.

Or maybe they weren't such little things. Like the fact that he seemed to notice everything.

Like just now, when the quality of the sunlight on his backpack made him draw up short in the middle of his preparations, one sock on and one sock off, and just stand there staring at it for a long moment. Appreciating its texture, and the ways it had begun to age, and feeling with a flash of intensity how his pack had come to feel like an extension of his body.

He went around looking at things as if he knew he would probably never see them again. He was hungry to capture every last detail. He figured that it was probably a pretty weird way for a guy his age to be looking at the world, but he was grateful for the sharpened perspective. As much as he wanted to capture and preserve it in song, he didn't want to miss a minute of it. To spend time on living his life or to spend time trying to immortalize the moments of his life in lyrics? He acutely felt the ancient dilemma.

Colin had developed a simple routine for starting the day in a new place. First, he'd work, without stirring from his room, for at least two hours, sometimes longer if the juices were flowing. He was conceptualizing the whole album, filling in elements that he felt were missing, rearranging tracks, and finessing transitions. The disciplined work done, he'd head out to find a suitable source for a cup of coffee and a bite of breakfast. Then, he'd choose a venue where he could set himself up with a gig for the night. And with those essential tasks accomplished, he'd be free to conduct what he thought of as the sonic research, and head off with his notebook to spend whatever was left of the day following the inclination of his ears and his feet around the city.

Juliet had given him a head start. Several of the bars she'd shown him would do the trick nicely, and he knew which one he wanted to try first, if he could only find it again. He felt more disoriented in Salamanca than he would have if he'd explored it for himself, without a guide. As it was, he'd been so caught up in paying attention to his companion that he wasn't sure at all where the bar called Macondo was in relation to where he'd ended up finding a place to stay at the late hour.

It didn't take more than a second for him to decide, as he laced up his boots, that he'd simply retrace his steps. He'd go back to the Plaza de la Libertad, where he and Juliet had ended their evening together, and trust his senses to lead him to Macondo from there. He slung his guitar over his shoulder, locked the room, went down the narrow stairs, and left the clunky old-fashioned key with the innkeeper.

As he made his way across the center of town he wondered whether he might see Juliet again, seated in the same café. It wasn't impossible. It was a relatively small town, and she obviously had her routines, too.

Colin had been traveling alone for awhile, but even casting back to the stretch of time before his departure, he couldn't remember having fallen so easily into someone's company, or enjoying it so much. Still, though his eyes sought the place and sought, too, the door to her building, by the time he'd reached the little plaza, he'd firmly resolved against the temptation to stake her out by having his morning coffee at that café. However enjoyable the evening, the good-bye had been definitive. It was all just good fodder for his lyrical work.

It turned out to be a simple matter for him to find his way from the Plaza de la Libertad to the Paseo de las Carmelitas, which he remembered as the ring road which marked a boundary around the old center of town. From there, with a bit of hit and miss, he soon found the Plaza del Oeste. He followed one of the streets that radiate out from the circular plaza, and found Macondo on Calle Jaime Vera.

All of the places that the lovely American woman had shown him were evidence of her discriminating eye for good venues. Most had interesting architectural features, and some were wildly popular, with crowds spilling from their doors into the streets. Macondo was immediately appealing on the basis of its name alone, evoking as it did Colin's vivid memory of the magic and wonder of *One Hundred Years of Solitude*—Rebeca with her bag of bones, *cloc-cloc*, and Remedios the Beauty surrounded by butterflies. But Colin was a savvy businessman, as well as a romantic, and he'd identified Macondo as his top choice for three practical reasons.

First, though there was nothing terribly interesting about its architecture, it had an open floor plan, which meant that a musician could set himself up in the corner near the window and be both visible and audible throughout the bar, as well as to anyone happening to pass by on the street. Second, from what he could assess during the course of the beer that they'd drunk there, the repertoire of music that the barman had chosen to set the tone for the evening was compatible with the sets that Colin was most comfortable playing. And, third, though the bar was populated with cool-looking clusters and pairs of young people engrossed in each other or listening to the music, the barman was far from being too busy to wonder how he might be doing better.

Colin recognized that particular look in the man's eyes. It was something midway between gratification that his place was hip enough to attract and hold these particular customers—with many of whom he was on a first-name basis--and anxiety that the place wasn't packed with people buying drink after drink, making his own time pass more fluidly and, more importantly, filling his cash register.

The same man was still there now, as Colin had hoped he might be, hunched over a newspaper behind the bar. At this hour of the day, the place had only three customers. A group of young women was drinking coffee and conversing without pausing for breath.

Carrying his guitar case in front of him like a calling card, Colin approached the bar directly and made his pitch. The proposition was straightforward: Colin would play and sing for a couple of hours. He'd draw and keep a thirsty crowd, satisfaction guaranteed. In return, the barman would proffer a tip jar "for the hungry musician" after every transaction.

By the time Colin closed with an offer to play something now, to persuade the man of his ability, it wasn't necessary. He had a knack for establishing an immediate rapport. Over a *café con leche*, the two men talked about music and women and food and about nothing. When other customers came in and interrupted them, it already felt as much like a new friendship as a business arrangement in which no one had anything to lose and both had something to gain.

"*Bueno, Paco, te dejo. Nos vemos a las once.*"

"*Hasta las once, chico. No te preocupes, que te guardo bien la guitarra.*"

With the evening's arrangements made and his hands free—he'd left his guitar safely stowed behind Paco's bar—Colin let himself wander. Salamanca by day didn't seem to have quite the same sparkle that it had the night before. In the strong sunlight, the streets looked dusty and the warm sandstone color of the buildings was washed out, over-bright. There were not a lot of people out and about, and those who were out moved with a less vibrant pace and sense of purpose.

Colin wondered why he wasn't feeling the excitement that he usually felt when he had a new place to explore. The weather was too warm, the streets were too dusty, the storefronts were too mundane. It didn't take him long to realize that, night or day, the city was not going to live up to the experience that he'd had of it with Juliet. Meeting her like that, as soon as he'd stepped off the train, and then spending uninterrupted hours in her company, had made the city glow for him. The sparkle that he missed was her company.

His perfect traveling companion would be as captivated as he was by the sight of a whole little troop of diminutive nuns in habits filing into the bus station. She would be as excited as he was to note that the year engraved on the burnished manhole covers along an entire block was 1903.

But after touring around town with Juliet, his imaginary companion was a poor substitute. He'd been wholly absorbed in their easy back and forth, her quick smile, the warmth of her presence—the delightful unexpectedness of the details that she pointed out to him. It had been so easy to fall into step with her.

Instead of observing the quirks and minutiae of the city while he walked, as he usually did, Colin was distracted by the memory of her face. It had glowed more warmly than the night-lit sandstone of the Plaza Mayor. And yet, he couldn't fix upon her features. She had been so animated, she slipped from the frame.

Absurdly, he found himself watching the sidewalks for her. She might appear anywhere! Absurdly, he imagined things he might say if he saw her. The right words escaped him.

Halfway across a busy street, in front of the only round church he'd ever seen, he laughed out loud at himself, drawing sharp glances from the pedestrians crossing towards him. To think that it had never occurred to him that he might be lonely. The first woman he spends time with in weeks, and he was stricken like a foolish schoolboy.

There was an easy song in this somewhere. Colin spied a small bar just behind the round church that had set up tables outside in the street. He sat down and took out his notebook. However unusual it was for him, he knew that there was something universal about this absurd feeling.

He understood that the trick lay in representing the universal and familiar in unique terms. *She wasn't just anybody, but I guess she could've been anybody, my lonely heart on the street skipped a beat.* He jotted down thoughts as they came, without second-guessing or permitting his obsession with the perfect to get in the way of anything that might turn out to be good.

Never mind the ring, she brings my heart around, a face I can't ever see, but won't forget. He became absorbed in his project quickly. He took little notice of the shifting of light along the curved side of the Iglesia San Marcos, and hardly looked up when he asked the *camarero* to bring him another coffee. The lyrics never satisfied him. He punctuated, emphasized, and persuaded with musical notation, sketched in drum fills and soaring strings. He'd had the blues for a moment, struggled to turn the feeling into a scheme of sound, and the afternoon flew into evening on ecstatic wings.

3

In the long rays of the setting sun, the city's stone façades warmed again to their golden glow. With hours still to go before his gig at Macondo, Colin got up to resume his exploration. With a kind of amazement at himself, and with no effort to resist, he began by finding his way back to the Plaza de la Libertad.

The tables at the little café where he'd met Juliet the day before were empty. He stood in front of the glass door of her apartment building. The building had four floors, with three apartments on each floor. Each had its own little silver button on the intercom. He imagined ringing first one and then the other. He paced back and forth three times, humming an air from an old musical. *All at once am I several stories high.* His memory held glimpses of her face, her eyes, her warmth beside him in the press of the crowd. But he remembered, with static and unfractured clarity, the ring on her finger. He felt his feet on the pavement again, and turned his steps away.

4

Juliet started her day much later than usual. She rose and dressed and then sat to write in her diary. She hesitated for a few minutes with her pen in her hand, running through the events and feelings of the previous afternoon, evening, and night in her mind's eye. She decided to record the truth of her experience and as she put her pen to the page, she knew clearly that this was no longer a diary that she would be sharing with anyone.

She saw no alternative. She was not going to censor her own experience. For her, that would be a breach of faith and a failure of science. The only way to keep true to her original intention, of keeping a diary of her experiences that she would share with Brad upon her return home, would have been to spend the previous day differently. And that, Juliet realized as she wrote, was an option that had only briefly crossed her mind, and that she had dismissed as an entirely different sort of breach of faith.

To turn aside from another experience that her heart felt alluring— that would be just like following Brad inside from the twilight and the fireflies again. She wondered how much more of herself she had been leaving behind, outside. She tried to apply a botanical analogy in order to understand herself better. She had been so ready to plant her heart, but just didn't know enough about how fast she'd grow, the kind of nutrients and light that she'd need, or the shape and form she'd take. By the time Juliet stopped writing—pressed, now, to get to her class on time—she was in an entirely unexpected frame of mind.

She knocked on Greta and Magda's door on her way downstairs, as always. When Magda opened, Juliet blurted out an awkward, "Hi! Er…good morning!" instead of her usual cheery "Buenos días."

Magda, smiling, raised an eyebrow.

"Oh, no! I've left my things. Back in a minute!" Juliet turned again and ran up the stairs to retrieve her book bag.

When she returned a moment later, Magda and Greta were waiting for her on the landing. Magda took her arm as they went down the stairs together.

"There's a dear," Magda said to her. "You're a bit discombobulated this morning. Are you feeling alright?"

"Yes, I'm fine. I think I'm just. Distracted." Juliet felt herself flush.

Greta looked at her closely, with her rheumy brown eyes, and it was her turn to raise an eyebrow.

"Our Juliet is not quite herself today."

"Or perhaps she is more herself than ever."

On other mornings, as the three American women walked across the Plaza Mayor together and down the narrow cobblestoned street to the Academia, they made small talk in two languages, reminding each other of new vocabulary words and pointing out sights of interest to each other. On this morning, by the time they were halfway across the Plaza, both of the elderly sisters knew that there was something troubling their younger companion.

Juliet was, indeed, distracted. She couldn't help herself. Her eyes restlessly scanned the streets, looking for the handsome young man with the long chestnut-colored hair.

By the time they'd reached their destination, the big building on the edge of the bluff above the Tormes, Juliet had driven herself nearly frantic with frustration. She could find no trace of the sharp focus that she normally brought with her to class. She acutely felt the imminence of her departure and her return home. She pictured her reunion with Brad, and felt guilty and disappointed in herself that she wouldn't be able to share the thoughtful diary that she'd been keeping. She had taken off her ring before showering, and had forgotten to put it back on her finger, which was very unsettling. And in a bewildering cross-current of thought, she was kicking herself for not having found out where Colin was going to be spending the night. She hadn't even found out how long he was planning to be in Salamanca. The town was just small enough that she couldn't keep herself from hoping she'd see him at every corner. But it was more than possible, she realized with a terrible emptiness—an emptiness that she told herself sternly was juvenile and foolish—that she would simply never see him again.

5

Juliet remained distracted throughout the day. Magda and Greta, with growing concern, were not the only ones to notice. Several of the teachers noticed as well.

"*¿Qué le pasa a nuestra Julieta hoy? ¿Demasiada marcha anoche? ¿O, se habrá enamorada con uno de nuestros chicos salmantinos por fin?*"

Juliet understood enough to blush and shake her head. But she couldn't reply. She was tongue-tied, and absorbed in thought. She could hardly bring herself to pay attention, and at various points wished that she had taken a sick day.

By the time classes ended, she had recovered herself to some degree. She had mentally resolved the problem of Colin. He had thrown her for a loop. But he was gone. A phenomenon, merely, like an unusual bit of weather. *Una llovizna de verano, un flechazo.*

What remained with her, was the problem of Brad. And the problem of not having kept up with the pace of her own growth.

"We're anxious about you, my dear," Greta said, taking her arm as soon as they left the building.

"You're plainly in some kind of distress," Magda added, taking her other arm.

"Why don't you tell us about it?

"Yes, do. We've been around the block a few times. We've got loads of perspective to spare."

"But take your time."

"And if we're prying, just say so."

Juliet smiled at her two friends as they began their walk across town. She had to think a bit before being able to find the right words for what was troubling her.

"What if…"

"Go on, dear."

"What if there's a little part of me that's…only fully alive when I'm not with Brad? What if that little part of me is maybe not so little? What if I can feel it growing, now that I'm so far away. And what if it feels more and more like *me*?"

6

Greta gave her arm another squeeze. "Maybe Magda will tell you the story about the time she broke off her engagement to marry a certain young naval officer."

For a story of lost love told by an eighty-something year old woman who had been living with her sister for over fifty years, it was not at all as sad as Juliet might have expected. Magda's watery eyes sparkled with life and certainty as she spoke about the unexpected decision that she had made at the age of twenty-five, when she realized that she was not ready to marry the handsome and self-assured young lieutenant.

"You see, I understood that a good marriage properly depends on some surrender of the self, and that some of us may stand to grow into something greater by giving up some of our self-centeredness. The trick, though, is recognizing the difference between two people making each other grow, and one person just letting herself shrink and disappear."

"Sisters living together can make each other grow, too, we've found."

"And there's never been any risk of one of us disappearing into the other."

"No, there hasn't."

With that, Magda and Greta shared a look in which Juliet could read a dozen layers of mutual understanding and opposition at once. They had shared two independent lifetimes: of frustration and gratitude, mischief and forgiveness.

7

Tired from her late night, after closing her apartment door behind her and dropping her bag on the tiled floor, Juliet threw herself onto the bed. *Me voy a echar una siesta,* she said aloud with a kind of rebellious lassitude. The *siesta* was not her usual late afternoon habit.

She slept deeply, and woke up with the evening well-advanced. She felt refreshed and had new insight into the late-night culture that she'd been observing without fully experiencing for herself.

It took her longer than usual to do her homework. She was distracted by the rapid approach of her departure date, and by thoughts of whether she had gotten the most out of her Salamanca experience. She had deliberately chosen to return again and again to the same café in the Plaza de la Libertad, while other foreign visitors chose to roam around the city, with an endless appetite to try a *café con leche* or a *vino tinto* in dozens of different places. Juliet had chosen one spot, close to her apartment, thinking that what she wanted was not to range about like a tourist, but to deepen, and to become part of a place, if only for a little while. And through that deliberate deepening, here she was, suddenly drawn to range beyond any desire or expectation.

When she imagined her return to Kansas City, and the hug with which Brad would greet her at the airport, she felt so anxious that she felt her breathing get shallow and her chest constrict. Brad's arms were strong, but he had never really held all of her.

Juliet had very thoughtfully chosen to study in Spain on account of both the language and the cultural history. She had tried articulating the scope of her ambition to Brad once or twice, but had ultimately been silenced by a look on his face that she interpreted as incredulity. Her parents had listened, though. And they had egged her on, just as they'd always done, ever since she'd been a little girl with wild extra-planetary visions inspired by Bruce Dern in *Silent Running*.

She had always thought as long as she could into the future. She knew that Mexico, and Central and South America were gigantic under-exploited gardens. And she knew that two things that all of those nations had in common were the Spanish language and the shared cultural history of being Spanish colonies. So, she had decided to supplement the graduate studies in botany that would allow her to pursue her notions and intuitions about sustainable agriculture with some knowledge of Spanish and of the root culture that all of those nations shared.

Someday, her understanding of the way the world worked would prevail. She just knew it, and could not conceive of a way that she could be wrong about it. It might be sugar, it might be coffee, or it might be grapes for wine or for the table. It might, in some nearly conceivable future, even be coca leaves or marijuana, or some other indispensable and obvious plant. Bananas! Avocados! Asparagus!

Whatever the exact crop, or crops—it would probably be crops—she knew that a gigantic North American or worldwide market would open up, and that it might open up particularly wide for agricultural methodologies that would be respectful of resource limitations, and of the imperative that there be some kind of acceptable level of livelihood for the laborers who made scaled agriculture possible. She thought of it as something like ecology, or mindful farming, or sustainability.

With her graduate studies, she would go after the science. And, by going to Spain, she'd get an edge on the language, and on the cultural roots that would give her some kind of fluency throughout an entire hemisphere of partner and customer relations. Her parents had listened, with the same look of appreciative awe that they'd had on their faces the first time she had insisted on going head first down their neighborhood's sledding hill. Brad had just pulled on her arm, and led her to the sofa so that they could resume watching their movie.

Juliet had always let Brad pull her away. There was some comfort in it. There was certainly some comfort in his strong arms. She let herself subside into that comfort, surrendering something, not entirely unwillingly. It occurred to her now that there was part of her that was ready to back away from some kind of an immense challenge, in favor of an easier, more familiar path.

She had flattered herself by thinking of it as a kind of humility. In this colder light of distant reflection she saw, with some alarm, that it might be fairer to attribute her surrender to slothfulness.

But now, Juliet had been strengthened by her independence and emboldened by the fact that she had made her own way to the Old World, where she was thriving. She was resolved to take on every challenge that presented itself.

She slipped out of her *siesta*-rumpled clothes, and put on a white cotton skirt and a sleeveless navy-blue silk blouse. It was warm in her room, and she knew that it would be no less warm on the streets. She slipped her feet into her sandals, sprayed a little perfume into the air, and stepped into it.

Except for the perfume, her actions were automatic. Throughout the length of her stay, she had never failed to make herself get out for a walk before bedtime.

Most nights, she contented herself with taking a few turns around the Plaza Mayor, or making her way to the Catedral Nueva and back. She always began by taking a turn or two around her own Plaza de la Libertad. This was a meditative practice for her. The night sky was purple above the flood-lit façades of the crenellated buildings. Before going anywhere else, she liked to take the time to absorb details about her immediate neighborhood: this special place where she had taken herself to live for the summer.

Still distracted, she was unable to notice the greater darkness of the night sky. The *siesta* had disrupted her schedule, and she was beginning her walk hours later than usual. She had awakened with Magda's words stuck in her head. Shrink and disappear? However easy and comforting that might be, it was not at all what she wanted for herself.

What she wanted was to step out into brighter light, grow into something unexpected, into something deeper and larger than could fit into any of the old frames or planters that had held her before. Whatever it was, it had to be closer to what was truth for her, and consistent with some inarticulate commitment that she had made to herself long ago, that had been her compass.

"*No pierdas el norte.*" Magda had quoted the idiomatic phrase they'd learned in class some days earlier when she shared her story about the young naval officer. The teacher had said that the phrase was used as a reminder about not losing one's way. Don't lose track of where north is for you. She should have asked Magda more questions. Juliet felt like the needle on her compass was spinning, as if it had been rendered useless by some powerful magnet.

What was her north? She understood the implication of the admonition. If she could just hang on to north, she could make her way forward through all kinds of confrontation and unpleasantness. Magda hadn't said anything about unpleasantness. But there must have been unpleasantness. Juliet lost track of how many laps she'd taken around the small plaza.

How long had it taken Magda to make her decision? She hadn't said anything about this terrible sensation of urgency and discomfort and fear of loss. Just yesterday, Juliet had been just fine. And now...she could barely think. She passed the doorway to her apartment again and started another lap.

She had a sudden vision of herself walking laps around the tiny plaza all night long, like a crazy woman, and knew immediately that she didn't want it to get any later.

She knew she was not crazy. She knew more clearly than most what she wanted to do with her life. She knew, too, that the commitment she'd made to Brad was not compatible with the commitment she'd made to truth.

A few blocks away from her apartment was a *locutorio*. She went inside to ask for a *cabina*. She called Brad.

She realized that there was no way to do what she needed to do without going through with it. She had to just say something, like firing off a flare, and she'd have to feel whatever the feelings were going to be. But she told herself that she didn't need to feel responsible for making him understand.

"I'm very sorry, but I need to end our engagement." She hadn't thought it all the way through before placing the call, but there it was, and it was what had to be said.

His protests were feeble and far away and did not touch her. Across half the globe, she heard him splutter with half-formed questions. She felt completely detached as she stubbornly, almost robotically, repeated her simplest truths: "I've got to end our engagement." Then, Brad's tone became sharper.

"That's it? Five years together, and you're breaking up with me over the phone without a word of explanation? You're the one who's always got to explain everything."

"I'm sorry. It's got something to do with having planted myself in the wrong pot."

"The wrong pot? I can't believe this. Juliet? Have you been body-snatched?"

"No…I…"

"Have you met someone else? Is that it? We've always been honest with one another. Just tell me the truth. Tell me something!"

This time, Juliet heard something unfamiliar in Brad's voice. What she heard was pain and fear of loss. It cut her determined resistance to engaging in anything messy to ribbons.

"No, we haven't always been completely honest with one another. Or, I haven't always been honest with you. I've let you think that everything was perfect. And yes, if you must know, I met someone. Just yesterday. So he is not why. And you are not why. I am why."

"What? Why? I don't understand."

"Look. I'm sorry this seems wrong to you right now. But staying engaged seems wrong to me. And if it's wrong for me, it's not right enough for you."

"You are always right enough for me, even when you're wrong."

"That's what I always used to believe about you, too."

"Ouch."

"Sorry. I didn't…"

"So that's it, huh? She left for the Plaza de la Libertad, never to return?"

"I'm sorry, Brad. To clear my own head, I just needed to tell the little bit of truth that I can see. When I'm able to say more, I'll say more. I'm just not ready right now. So, this is goodbye."

"I don't accept this at all. I can't believe you're doing this again."

Juliet removed the receiver from her ear, and gently rested it in its cradle. That last remark had stung. *Again!* Once she had confessed to Brad that she'd broken up with her previous boyfriend the very same evening that Brad had first presented himself in her life.

She remained seated in the *cabina*, and let out a deep breath. Trying to stay true to some kind of north, Juliet told herself that breaking off her engagement was a renewal of her commitment to her own independence and future.

She thought of Magda and Greta, and then of her own sister, Jackie. She didn't ever need to be married. She would make her own way forward. Just the thought of how she might grow, what unexpected twists and turns her unbound life might take, filled her with strength and with a feeling of excitement that rose up in her like warm sap.

After another deep breath, when Juliet stood up and left the *cabina*, she felt like she was stepping into the sky. She had told some truth and felt at least partially restored to herself.

Without admitting to any clear purpose, she headed up the Calle Zamora, toward the edge of the city. She was traveling upstream, against the schools of young women dressed for an evening out who were making their way toward the Plaza Mayor. The sharp sounds of their heels provided staccato counterpoint to the chiming gaiety of their festive voices.

As she walked, Juliet took heightened pleasure in the warm breeze that wafted its way down the street toward the center of the city. She took pleasure, too, in the voices and bright glances and sleek black hair of the girls who passed her, caught up in their own worlds of anticipation and transition. She thought again about Santa Teresa's dusty sandals, and about what it means to have the direction of one's steps determined and drawn onward, through all kinds of challenges, great and small, by the electric pull of some inexpressible ecstasy. There were no fireflies at twilight in Salamanca. But the warm night air smelled of desert and stone and vibrated with laughter and music and raised voices.

Juliet did not think about where she was going. She took a single turn around the Iglesia de San Marcos, just to be there completely, and then crossed the ring road that marked the limit of the old city center. She walked up a short, narrow street lined with the nondescript apartment buildings that characterized so much of modern Salamanca, and then, as she stepped out into the round pool of light that was the Plaza del Oeste, she finally acknowledged with a mixture of dread and guilt and anticipation that she had an immediate destination after all. She'd had a feeling all along, and she simply couldn't help herself.

From the end of the street, she could see the green neon glow of the sign above the door: *Macondo*. Her mind supplied her with a memory of the novel's opening: when a father took his son on a long journey to see ice for the first time. A few steps later, she could hear a guitar. And then, Colin's voice, even more compelling than she'd imagined it might be, rang out in song above the laughter and conversation.

Suddenly, Juliet felt shy and uncertain. She had a moment's impulse to turn and walk away. "What am I doing here?" she asked herself. But there was no point in asking. She did not feel that there was a choice for her to make. She took a breath and stepped through the door.

8

The room was crowded. There were clusters of people gathered along the length of the bar and all of the tables were occupied. Juliet made her way to the end of the bar, where there was one empty stool. She ordered a *Mahou*. Colin would have to turn his head to his left to see her now. When he did, he couldn't possibly miss her on her perch. She sipped her beer. She crossed and uncrossed her legs nervously. And then she lost herself in the music.

Colin bent his head downward as he played his gleaming white guitar. A thick lock of his long hair hung over his face so that Juliet could not make out his expression. At first, she didn't recognize what he was playing. But she knew enough to hear at once that his musicianship was masterful. It had a simple, catchy pop beat, but Colin added offbeat accents that were distinctly reminiscent of flamenco.

The tune became familiar all of a sudden, and Juliet detected a shift in the attention of the crowd. Groups that had been talking before were now just listening in obvious appreciation.

When Colin began to sing, Juliet knew the song at once. It was a radio favorite that she'd been enjoying all summer, rendered acoustically now, and with a distinctive Spanish flavor. By the time he finished the song, the bar scene had been converted into a concert venue. Everyone was listening, and everyone applauded enthusiastically.

Colin looked up with a grateful smile. He pushed the hair out of his face. He turned his head to the left and, sure enough, spotted Juliet immediately.

His smile broadened as he nodded at her and doffed an imaginary cap. Juliet flushed and smiled back and waved her hand, drawing the sharply appraising glances of a couple of women on the other side of the room.

Colin began to play again. The tune was recognizable from the opening chords, drawing enthusiastic nods and sounds of appreciation from his audience. It was another radio favorite of the summer, but rendered so uniquely, and with such intimate understanding, that it seemed to give more back to the original than it derived.

With a tingling sensation in the pit of her stomach, Juliet realized that Colin was not just a summer busker. She wondered at his talent, and wondered if he had original material that he would share.

It was not easy for her to take her eyes off of him. When she did, she became distracted by the sight of all of the others in the crowd who were equally fixated. Colin was a natural and unconscious performer. While he bent his head downward to play his way through intricate passages, he lifted his face to sing. His emotive, yearning, sometimes comical, expressions added power to the lyrics. He raised his eyebrows, and pursed his lips. He occasionally raised a hand from the guitar to beckon or to pinch off a telling point.

All around the crowded room, women were watching him in rapture. They leaned forward with flashing eyes and parted lips, wholly forgetful of their male companions—who were themselves no less absorbed in this unexpected event.

Juliet saw that the attentiveness of this much larger crowd was as complete as it had been in the tiny bar of La Formentera the night before. But the quality of this attention was very different. In La Formentera, the feeling—however exotic to her—had been ritualized, familiar. The crowd breathing that flamenco air was reconnecting with some ancient, homogeneous part of itself. By native instinct, they stepped into the familiar forms of *sevillanas*, their hands beat in choral rhythms.

Here, in the otherwise featureless space of the Macondo, Colin's performance had pushed the entire room full of people into the unfamiliar. It was riveting and unsettling, and there would be no returning to it for any of them.

Colin ended one song and began another with hardly a pause to mark the transition, or to allow the crowd to express its appreciation with its burst of applause and cries of encouragement.

He was singing to her. Juliet was sure of it when their eyes met again for a moment, when she recognized his next tune as another she knew and loved.

In another moment, she was completely unsure, when she took in the crowd around her again and felt herself to be just an atomized one of this enthralled many. All were moths drawn to a single bright flame and feeling themselves to be uniquely enkindled.

When Juliet was eleven, her father and some of his old college friends had taken her to see The Rolling Stones at the International Amphitheatre. It was her first concert. She had only really just begun taking an interest in music. She didn't think of herself as a Stones fan. It was just something fun she was going out to do with her Dad while they were on vacation visiting family in Chicago. It felt like forever to get from the parking lot into the venue, and then, as it turned out, they were three rows from the stage.

She had felt electrified. These men whose names she hardly knew were not musicians so much as they were magicians. They reveled in their power on the stage, attracting a whole amphitheater full of moths to their bright light.

While singing "Love in Vain," Mick Jagger looked at her, she thought. Their eyes met for a second, she thought. She had felt a rush of heat, or cold. She distinctly thought, "so this is what they mean by going weak in the knees." And even as she retained her capacity for detached analysis, she felt tears on her cheeks.

A hungry hollow opened up inside her when he looked away and moved to the other end of the stage. She watched him set a whole other little crowd of moths aflutter.

But this Colin really was singing to her. She was sure of it again with the next song change. He pushed his lock of hair back and looked right at her. He smiled and shrugged and shook out his right hand. He was wearing himself out. He was plainly telling her. The end was coming soon. The whole crowded room would fall away then. They could head out into the night together.

And then...how could he know it? He began to sing one of her favorite songs. It was Elvis Costello's "Alison." It was like she was hearing the lyrics for the first time. She had never taken them so personally before. Now in the bright light of Colin's soft voice, Juliet felt that she had paused on the threshold of a future with a man who couldn't see that he left the best parts of her outside. Dust to magic dust. No aim had ever been more true.

The crowded room fell away completely for Juliet right then. Past and future fell away. She knew that she was no moth. Colin was drawn to her light, too. Even as she remained perched on her stool, she was elevated. They were in a glowing dust cloud of light together. They were distinct and separated from all the rest.

Part of Juliet would always remain perched there on that Macondo stool. Perched as if at the top of a roller coaster. She knew she was about to rush down into some tumultuous surge of feeling. She knew that she was letting go of things that she had almost allowed to define her.

And then the moment and the song were over. Time rushed like giddy water through a narrow passage. Colin unslung his guitar. He stood up. He made a quick, modest bow. The bar erupted in a commotion of applause and movement and calls for more music and replenished drinks. He packed his instrument in its case, and handed it to the barman who clapped him gratefully on the back and handed him a cold beer.

Salsa blasted from the bar's speakers. Dancing couples stepped in eagerly to fill the space that Colin had held clear. Colin shouldered his way through the standing, dancing crowd. He smiled and nodded as he was touched and patted by his appreciative audience. He stepped right up to where Juliet still sat on her perch. He placed his bottle of beer on the bar and held out his hand.

"Dance with me?"

The roller coaster started down. She put her hand in his and slipped off her stool.

They danced. The crowd was closely packed. His hand was on her hip, then held the small of her back. Their bodies pressed together and parted and pressed together again in Latin rhythm.

"You found me." His lips almost touched her ear.

He spun her out and back in again.

"I was afraid I wouldn't," Juliet heard herself say, her lips to his ear.

"I was afraid, too."

Holding hands, they made their way out into the street. The crowd had spilled out of the bar, and merged there with crowds from other bars. The flow of pedestrian traffic tended toward the Calle Zamora and the center of the old city. Colin and Juliet walked with the flow, holding onto each other's hands. It was one-thirty in the morning by the clock in the Plaza Mayor. The crowd was thicker than it had been at midday.

They walked on from there together, saying little, thinking their own thoughts. Colin had noticed right away that Juliet was not wearing her engagement ring. He wondered about this. She had come out to the Macondo alone, seeking him. He didn't know what this meant, or where it could or would lead. It was like having a single lyric or musical phrase. He recognized it as precious, but it didn't fit anywhere.

He didn't know how it could fit anywhere. He clung to her small, strong hand and studied her in sidelong glances, trying to impress her features upon his memory so that he'd be able to call them up accurately in her absence.

Her nose was not exactly as she would have liked, and she was never completely happy with her hair. She was self-conscious, and tended to worry that she might have food stuck in her teeth. Colin took every bit of her in, and thought she was perfect.

Juliet's head swirled. She had put Brad aside. However clumsily, it was long overdue. And then she had allowed herself, without fully formulated thought, to head out in search of this beautiful man with the locks of hair and the blue eyes, whose hand now held her own so tightly.

She knew that she wanted that hand in hers. She knew how she felt each time they bumped shoulders as they walked along together. She knew that she did not care what time it was. She was not ready to think about their moment of parting. She could not think about it.

She was alive and right where she wanted to be. She wished that she could stop time—her whole world remain in this faerie light.

They turned on to the Calle de Bordadores, and stopped in the pool of light and shadow beneath Pablo Serrano's monumental statue of Miguel de Unamuno, the philosophical hero of the city.

"My religion is to seek for truth in life and for life in truth," Juliet recited. "Even knowing that I shall not find them while I live."

"But don't we find them if we seek them? At least some of the time? If only briefly?"

"Does the truth always keep moving on?"

The truth tonight, Juliet imagined writing in her diary, *is that I went out hoping to find this man.* When he let go of her hand and moved to the other side of the statue, she felt cold in the pool of light. And, when he completed his orbit and returned to her side, reaching out for both of her hands with both of his, she shivered with a rush of warmth. *I don't know what I am doing*, she imagined writing. *I don't think I can help myself.*

She wanted to press up against him and feel, smell, his warmth. Her eyes kept returning to his lips.

Around the corner from the Unamuno monument, in a niche in the stone wall that lined the narrow street, was one of Juliet's favorite shrines to the Virgin. The brightly painted statue was illuminated by a single naked bulb.

My religion, she imagined she'd write. *Is suspended somewhere on a continuum between Unamuno and the Virgin Mary.* She wanted to remain true, above all, and to feel, at least sometimes, the overwhelming might of grace with her.

In what she had narrowly thought of as the Virgin's terms, remaining true was simple and impossible. She had betrothed herself to Brad. They were supposed to get married. They would have a house near both their families. They would have children together and everything would be as it should be, as they'd planned it to be. There was a pattern for her life and future growth with him. The Virgin, as she imagined her, would approve.

But in what Juliet acutely felt to be Unamuno's tragic terms, she could not feel the life in that avowed truth. She stood in the warm night air, beneath a canopy of the same bright stars she remembered from her home on the Midwestern plains, with uneven stones beneath her sandaled feet. That avowed truth was as false and garish and forced as the paint and ornaments on this street-side Virgin.

It seemed that nothing had ever felt as real to her as this present moment. Just being out and alive in the night, with music coming from somewhere close by, and feeling this irresistible force of attraction: it was untamed.

Juliet felt an unexpected sense of recognition, remembering fireflies and her legs dangling in the water of the lake at twilight. She'd never fully understood it before, that this is what it might feel like to be full of grace. This was life, her life. The truth she sought in it shone back at her in irregular pieces, gleaming tiles for a mosaic still in progress. If there was a pattern, she couldn't see it yet.

Piece by piece, she knew, life was composed of a sequential placing of moments. This new hand that she held in hers—bone, sinew, and muscle—held life and truth in it. Rather than pulling her away from herself, into artificial light and predetermined patterns, this new hand seemed to be tugging her to a deeper, unexplored, cell of her own interior castle, where inside opened up to an orbiting flight beneath a night sky full of stars.

"I think we have some more dancing we need to do tonight," she said, fixing her eyes on his.

Colin nearly kissed her then. She seemed so utterly familiar to him in that moment, standing in the narrow street beside the little shrine. The face he'd first seen in profile the day before, now turned with its full power of light shining directly upon him. Everything else faded and fell away into insubstantial shadow.

"Say no more." He tugged at her hand, pulling her toward the music around the corner.

Juliet laughed and Colin held on tighter. They made their way through the crowd inside the old convent-turned-dance club, and found a space of their own on the floor.

They danced together—arms and hands and hips and shoulders, pushing and pulling, laughter, and smiles, and brightly flashing eyes. Colin did not think of himself as a dancer, but this was different, a playful conversation.

Juliet felt like she was shaking off a hundred years. She was twenty three. Life and power coursed through her body. An observer of the Salamanca night no longer, she felt that detachment of hers drop away. She was caught up.

Song after song, they made seamless, joyous motion together. There was a break in the music. They clung to each other still, the world spinning on around them. Chest to chest, their faces a breath away.

Juliet felt her face glowing in the dance floor light, saw that Colin's face was glowing, too. Studying his lips, his smiling, bright teeth. To kiss, to dissolve into that light and warmth. She wondered and felt herself pulled as if by gravity.

Colin nearly kissed her then, too, but spoke instead.

"Thirsty? Tired? Hungry?"

"Maybe. Not at all. I don't know."

They laughed and felt each other's laughter.

They stepped into a quiet bar nearby. They ordered icy *cañitas* of Mahou, and small plates of *aceitunas* and *jamón Serrano*.

"Did you say that this is your last week here?"

"My flight home is on Thursday. I'll take the bus to Madrid early that morning."

"Four days, then."

During his months of travel, Colin had gotten used to time stretching ahead of him indefinitely. It was a resource that he measured only in terms of his progress back toward the recording studio.

"When are you going back?"

"I don't know. I don't have a plan yet. When I'm ready. Another month or two, maybe."

"And home? Where is home for you?"

"Los Angeles?" It was as much a question as an answer, always. "My...family is in the Bay Area."

Neither could wrap their heads around the conflicts of time and space. They wrapped their fingers around each other's fingers in the here and now.

They talked about where they'd been and what they'd seen. Both loved ancient structures, stained glass, church organs, farmers markets, and walking alone in all weather. Colin's descriptions of soundscapes made Juliet wish that she had been listening more closely during her stay in Salamanca. Juliet's fascination with history and agriculture and the lives of saints made Colin wish that he'd taken the trouble to populate his travels with more reading.

"I wish..."

"Go on."

"I wish I'd met you sooner, is all."

"Four days isn't very long."

"Maybe we can get time to just stop."

"We cannot make our sun stand still, yet we will make him run."

"A lyric?"

"An old poem by Andrew Marvell."

My perfect traveling companion, Colin thought.

"Let's run!"

They ran, laughing. Hand in hand at first, then Juliet broke away and sprinted ahead down an empty night street. Colin flew after her, and they clung to one another gasping to catch their breath.

They danced again, making their way from one club to the next, following the music. Their energy and attraction wove themselves into the fabric of the night—a young couple out amongst young couples, and bands of restless singles, too, grasping, yearning. The night was alive with feeling: hope and desire and a yawning abyss of hungry solitude all around.

The last bar of the night flashed on its bright lights to drive the crowd out into the street. Juliet and Colin swung along with the rest of them, late night troops of couples and clans clattering and singing their way up the Calle Zamora to the *chocolatería* which was just opening up for its booming business.

The pale lavender light of dawn was in the sky as they stood on the sidewalk smiling over *churros y chocolate*. This was what it was like to fall for a perfect stranger.

They were both thinking it. Both were thinking "perfect, perfect." And, "too bad about the impossible timing." Neither needed to say anything. There was nothing and no one and nowhere else for either.

PART FOUR

1

Looking back so many years later, Juliet saw that in a way time *had* stopped for her then. She had returned again and again to that span of time and always found it there intact—standing like a slender bridge that she had built and then crossed into what she ever after thought of as her adult life. She could recover those moments, and the turbulent rush of conflicted feelings that accompanied them, unfailingly.

Just as she stopped to admire certain works of architecture during her travels, Juliet examined that span of time at the end of her stay in Salamanca until she knew every buttress, bay, and pediment intimately. One perfect night with head and heart in turmoil populated hundreds of nights. That night became her reference point for all she'd ever pretend to know about what happens when irresistible attraction strikes at commitment and planning like a bolt of lightning from the heavens.

The morning people, on their way out for coffee and newspapers and cigarettes, had already begun to mix in the streets with the night people as Juliet and Colin made their way toward the center. In the Plaza de la Libertad there was no moment of hesitation, and no word exchanged. Juliet used a large key to open the heavy outer door. Colin looked at her with eyes and smile that were ready to say good night and good morning. Juliet reached out and pulled him inside, as simple as that.

He kissed her then. Or she kissed him. This point of agency was unclear, and remained unclear. Juliet came to think of it as a kind of micro-gravity. It had felt exactly like gravity. Two celestial bodies with overlapping orbits had passed close enough together that the invisible weight of their mass and energy annihilated the space between them, along with any need for personal agency, explicit query, or consent.

The sound of an apartment door opening in the stairwell above them interrupted their embrace. Juliet took Colin's hand and led him upstairs. There was a moment of fumbling. Her hands trembled as she used a smaller key to open the door to her little apartment. And then they were inside with the door closed behind them.

Pink dawn filtered in through the gauzy curtain covering the single window. There was no need to turn on the light. Juliet pressed herself against him, taut warm skin smelling of sweat and tobacco and chocolate.

They kissed again while standing there. Juliet put a cassette tape—her eclectic ballad mix—in the little portable player she'd bought for herself within a few days of her arrival. They danced in the narrow space between her single bed and her desk. Slow dancing, the way they'd both learned to do in high school, or middle school, with their bodies pressed closely together and simply shuffling in slow revolutions while the entire tape played itself through.

The sun was well up by then. Their long night had caught up with them. There was no thought of parting. Juliet sat down on her bed, and pulled Colin after her. They lay back, fully clothed. Juliet nestled into the crook of his arm and rested her head on his chest.

She took a last few deep, quiet, breaths, filling her head with the blend of scents that had accumulated on him over the course of their night together. With her last dim flickering of consciousness, she thought of her diary entry for the day: "and then I fell asleep in his arms." And so she did.

Juliet woke up first. She was happy to lie there. Her head was on his chest, she could feel it rising and falling with his breath. Her body was in contact with his along its entire length.

Her head filled with powerful, wanton urges. She found herself contemplating the two layers of clothing that separated them with an animal frustration that was wholly unfamiliar to her. She wanted to undo his every last button, and feel skin on skin.

She could hardly believe herself, and her body started shaking as she tried to stifle the burst of laughter that rumbled up out of some deep place inside her. It was no use. Colin felt her shaking and woke up.

"What's so funny? Do you always wake up laughing?"

Juliet snorted, and they both laughed.

"Shh!" she said, and let her fingers start to undo his shirt buttons.

They made a couple of half-hearted attempts to part ways as the morning progressed. Their orbits had intersected, but their trajectories were completely distinct. They both knew that they had to let go.

But instead they kept falling back onto Juliet's little bed, clinging to each other. Juliet's fingers found the callouses on Colin's fingers and traced them. Colin's lips whispered across her cheeks and chin, memorizing. One topic followed another. Colin pulled his socks on and put one of his feet into a boot.

Juliet had relieved herself of any obligation to Brad. But she still had a flight out of Madrid to catch in just a few days. And the start of her graduate program loomed not long after that. She had been on a steady, sensible roll toward a completely unobjectionable future.

And now, just as her forward momentum was intensifying, she couldn't bring herself to get out of bed for longer than it took for her to get up and pee. With the door open. So that there was not even that little moment's restoration of her separate identity.

She washed her hands, looked up, and saw herself in the mirror. It was the oddest sensation. Her hair was mussed. Her eyes were bright and clear. She could see the reflection of the open door behind her, and through it, the rays of afternoon sunlight, cut by shadows, on the wall. Colin, this warm, beautiful boy, Colin, was saying something about a waterfall in the north of England that he'd had to pay a fee in a pub to be able to see.

Without vanity, or even much awareness of herself, Juliet gazed at the pretty girl she was seeing in the mirror. For as long as she could remember, she'd had the sharpest sense of time as something that she invested carefully in order to yield a desired return in the future.

But now she was just looking at a living girl whose only consideration for the future was that as soon as she turned around and stepped back out of the bathroom she could press herself up against this beautiful boy's warm body and drink another luscious kiss from his sweet mouth.

Beyond that, she couldn't formulate a coherent thought. It was quite a sensation.

Finally, just before four in the afternoon, they left Juliet's apartment together. After a few empty gestures and unfinished sentences, they'd given up any notion that the next right thing for them to do was to part ways and to resume their distinct trajectories. Their first stop was the little travel agency a few blocks away. Juliet changed her airplane ticket to an open-ended return. There was no discussion beforehand. She had just pulled him along with her, saying that there was something that she needed to do. Thinking that she was doing it for herself, for her independence, not for him. All it took was a few minutes and a fifty dollar fee that she was happy to put on her credit card.

For the next three days they were inseparable. The farthest apart they got was when Colin returned to the Macondo each night to play for growing crowds. Even then, Juliet sat on a bar stool and watched and listened from across the room. She was absorbed in the exhilarating present moment, in the strength of this new connection, in her free flight from the boundaries that she'd set for herself.

It was as if she had been one person and was now another person, living in another dimension. Time was too precious and fast-moving to turn away from what was presenting itself to her so compellingly, or to spend any of it writing in her diary. But she thought often of what she would try to write, and wondered if she could ever find words to represent this powerful feeling of attraction, and her commitment to not allowing it to signify anything beyond the moment, without making herself seem completely shallow and heartless.

She didn't feel shallow or heartless. She felt like she had fallen into deep, deep water and that her heart had grown to fill her chest. She felt like she was swimming strong in her own element for the first time in her life. This is what is real, she kept thinking. Everything changes. Nothing is permanent. This is what is true.

All of her senses joined forces, drowning out the small voice that wanted to remind her of Brad, of that story with a future in which she'd cast herself, and intrude on what was manifesting itself as real with questions about commitment and temptation. *How could you? Who are you?* They were the only words the small voice could get her to hear. *How could I not?* was her steady response. And, *I am a real person who must live a real life.*

She kept catching glimpses of herself in shop windows and puddles. Surprised by these appearances of a familiar looking stranger, she was possessed by an incredible, unexpected joy. There was a beautiful, strong, and independent young woman who might catch anyone's eye. She moved with grace against a backdrop of scenes from a city that she'd chosen for herself, so familiar and foreign, with its rooftop crowds of silver television antennae, its eroded stone, its well-dressed men and women. She held a beautiful young man's hand in hers.

She didn't just feel like she was going places, here she *was*—having gotten herself to places, and with so many places to get to and not a minute wasted. She was never again going to let someone pull her away from that faerie light.

This young man Colin showed no signs of doing that. Half the time she was pulling him along, holding his hand in hers as he came along willingly right beside her. He pulled her, too, but it was always to see more of the light.

His hand tightened on hers and tugged. When she turned toward him, Colin just lifted his chin and pointed upwards with his eyes. Her eyes paused for just a second on his smiling lips, and then she saw what he was seeing. The upper quarter of the Catedral Nueva's massive tower was distinctly off-kilter.

"Why haven't I noticed that before?"

"There was a big earthquake in Lisbon in 1753. I read something about it on the train. A lot of people died. It shook hard here in Salamanca and damaged the tower."

"Lisbon is far away."

"The earth moved. Without a warning. It was about a minute ago, in the grand scheme of things."

"Have you ever been in an earthquake?"

"Sure. What's amazing is how easy it is for everyone to forget how common they are in California. Massive forces are on the move all the time."

"We think we're so in charge of what happens to us."

"And then...we don't just act surprised. We really are surprised. We really think that we're going to see all our plans through, that it's up to us. That all it takes is determination."

Juliet saw something in Colin's face then that she hadn't noticed before. Some kind of reckoning or sorrow in his eyes or in the corners of his eyes, in the set of his lips at rest.

"Hey," she said, beginning to form a question.

But he smiled then and kissed her, and she had no space left inside for anything so empty as past and future.

Juliet and Colin walked and talked for hours on the afternoon of their fourth day together. As the sun approached the horizon, they reached the abrupt western edge of the city and followed an unpaved road past the cemetery to the top of the highest hill for miles around.

The city with its spires and walls was shrunken and self-contained in the immensity of the Castilian plain. The Sierra de Gredos marked the southern horizon. Salamanca had been a key site on the *ruta de la plata*—the trade route which carried tin from the mines in Astorga all the way to Merida—since before the Romans.

All those thousands of years of history, and yet the spot where Juliet and Colin stood alone together admiring the panorama had remained free of any human structure. It seemed incredible to them. The hillside was rich with the smell of thyme in the cooling air of the end of the day. It was the only vegetation in that dry place, but it was abundant and they could not keep from crushing it underfoot.

It was nearly dark as they made their way back down into the city. They were both elated. Though he hadn't really believed that she existed, Colin seemed to have found his perfect traveling companion. They talked of all the places they might go together. Juliet felt powerful and free and looked ahead into the unknown with a degree of excitement that she'd forgotten she was capable of feeling.

They finally parted ways, for the first time since Colin had pulled her off her bar stool after his performance, in the center of the Plaza Mayor. Juliet had made plans to meet up with Magda and Greta, who would be leaving for Madrid the next morning without her. Colin had a head full of lyrical fragments to put down on paper. The plan was to meet up again in three hours, at Juliet's apartment. Just three hours. Still, letting go of each other's hands, after a lingering kiss, felt like a tearing in half.

2

Magda and Greta were waiting for her at one of the outdoor tables at the Café Novelty in the corner of the plaza. As she walked up, Juliet realized that her parting from Colin had been in plain view for them, if they'd been watching for her in the crowd.

Before sitting down, she bent over to exchange *dos besos* with each of them, feeling the tissue papery-soft skin of their cheeks against her own. Then, rather than prolonging any awkward uncertainty, she took a deep breath and plunged right in with it.

"So, I've met a fellow."

"So we've seen," Greta said, as Magda nodded. Both pairs of eyes were wide as saucers.

"He's an American. A musician. I called off my engagement to Brad." She felt it was important to clarify. A matter of propriety.

"Over the telephone?"

"How did that go?"

"It was awkward. And liberating."

"I remember," said Magda. "Though I ended my engagement in person, and I wasn't leaving him for another man."

"I…" Juliet faltered, stung by this unfavorable comparison. She felt heat rising in her face, and her lower lip trembled. The elation and utter joy she'd been feeling in Colin's arms scarce moments before drained away as she was reminded of Brad's stinging remark, and of her history of failure.

"I'm sorry, dear," Magda hastened to add, placing her bony, veiny old lady's hand on Juliet's. "That didn't come out right."

"We're not at all judgmental," Greta added helpfully.

"I just meant to say that I felt liberated because my naval officer, so charming and handsome, was like a cozy, velvet egg. I could've stayed inside there. That could've been me. But I had to hatch."

"You wanted to learn to fly on your own."

Magda nodded, smiling in complicity with her sister. "I saw my sister learning to fly, and wanted to do that, too."

"Choosing to be a single woman was very unusual back in the day."

"We felt very bohemian."

Despite the sisters' warmth and good intentions, Juliet felt diminished and shaken. Was she just going to move from one man to another and never experience the liberation that Magda and Greta had known for most of their lives? She'd been telling herself that she'd set herself free, but she'd attached herself to another companion.

The conversation turned to easier things. Juliet made a credible effort to regain her composure, not wishing to make the sisters feel that they had upset her. But even as she chattered amiably with them about the highlights of their summer and their expectations regarding the months ahead, she remained stuck on questions about the nature of liberty and love.

And truth! She had such strong feelings about truth, about being honest with herself, at least. Even when circumstances made it seem impossible or unreasonable to be completely truthful with others, Juliet was strict in shunning self-deception.

In every difficult moment and situation she'd always reminded herself to search for a truth that she could grasp, even if sometimes all she could find was only a tiny finger hold. She knew that even the tiniest truth was part of the all-encompassing truth of reality which was too big and complex in its movements and configurations for her to see or understand. When the fog of her life was like the fog of war, with bewildering sounds and sensations and dangers all around, the best she could do was feel with blind fingers for whatever little ledge or crevice or fault-line of truth and cling on for dear life. All the rest was faith.

The truth was that she had not been unaware of feeling something less than wildly excited and completely fulfilled by her relationship with Brad. Why, then, had she waited to break up with him until she felt this irresistible pull of attraction from another?

Brad was right. As he'd reminded her with his barbed remark, she'd done it before. What he didn't know, because she was too ashamed to admit it to him or anyone else, was that she'd done the same thing not once, but two times before. Twice, she had put an end to one thing only once she'd felt the unmistakable beginning of something else. She had traded up.

Each time, she'd told herself that she was leaving something unreal behind for the sake of something real. Each time, she'd told herself that she was heeding the call of a disruptive and unorthodox higher power that exposed the fraudulence of self-imposed rules.

Each time, she'd called Shakespeare's old sonnet to mind, interpreting her higher commitment to true love as justification for her inconstancy. Love is not love which alters when it alteration finds. Oh no. It is an ever fixed mark. She must've been wrong, she'd told herself, and now she was being corrected. What she had called love was not love, for it had altered.

Love, the tidal force, advanced and receded, leaving her scoured and exposed. Again, something like gravity, it pulled her towards itself, respectful of no human barrier built on a misperception.

That was exactly the story she'd told herself on those two other occasions. Now, she resolved again, strengthened and inspired by the example of these two wise older women, she was not going to allow herself to believe it.

Having parted ways with Colin, and having finally put an end to her tired old commitment to Brad, Juliet felt as if she'd been released from a spell. If love was going to expose her heart, again and again, as being fickle and traitorous, then she was going to proceed henceforth in a more scientific manner and treat her perceptions of love with great suspicion.

The start of her graduate program at Cornell was seven weeks away, glimmering steadily on the horizon. It was a major navigational beacon on the course that she'd set for herself. By changing her return flight, she'd impulsively bought herself some free time to spend with this alluring young man from whom she could not yet bear to part. But nothing would stand in the way of her commitment to her own future. The goodbye was coming.

Magda and Greta each held one of Juliet's hands as the three women stood together on the platform outside the door to the sisters' apartment. They had lingered over coffee, and had then taken several laps around the Plaza Mayor before making their way back to the building where they'd spent the best part of their summer.

"You are growing such beautiful wings," said Greta.

"Please write and tell us about all of the places they'll carry you," urged Magda, squeezing her hand.

"I'm sorry I won't be traveling to Madrid with you in the morning, as we'd planned." As she said it, Juliet tried to imagine a ghost of herself carrying her bags and boarding the *Autores* bus. But the ghost was too wispy to last even long enough for her to picture the bus closing its doors.

"I think it's thrilling that you've changed your plans."

"The immediate future is a complete mystery to me right now." Juliet shook her head with misgiving as she spoke.

"To know that! Not to have already populated even tomorrow with plans and expectations!" Greta closed her eyes and shivered.

"Thrilling," her sister repeated, nodding with enthusiasm.

Juliet embraced each of them. She felt the strength of her own arms and shoulders in contrast with the frail skeletons which seemed almost to poke through the thin sweaters which had been a regular feature of their wardrobes through the weeks of summer.

"*Buen viaje, mis amigas. Muchísimas gracias por todo lo que habéis compartido conmigo,*" Juliet said. "I promise I'll write." She turned and waved, and climbed the next flight of stairs toward her apartment.

Once inside, Juliet closed the door behind her and stood with her back against it. The cozy little room would only be hers for another day. If she wanted to stay longer, she'd have to go upstairs and knock on the landlady's door. Chances were good, she figured, that she'd be out of luck. She'd reserved the space herself a full month before her arrival.

But the prospect of not knowing where she might be sleeping the next night didn't make her at all uneasy. She had cast off the old moorings—that childish engagement! She felt strong and ready for the unknown. She had nearly a thousand dollars in traveller's checks, a credit card, a passport, a substantial level of comfort with Spanish, and every belonging she needed pared down to what fit easily in bags that she could perfectly well manage for herself. It was truly, as the sisters had said, thrilling.

The front door buzzer rang, startling her. *Colin!* She reached for the receiver which hung on the wall beside her, was about to pick it up. Stopped herself in time, to observe.

She felt that pull, away from herself, away from the moment's reverie of freedom…she had only just dipped her toes in! And now, here was this new young man come to call.

Never mind that this was the plan that they'd agreed upon when they parted in the plaza. That was before she'd had a chance to recover herself, to reconnect with her emerging sense of independence.

The anticipated thrill of making her own way forward competed with her compulsion to respond to the buzzer, to not keep him waiting, to find out, and right away, if that feeling that she'd felt with him would carry her altogether away again. She observed the swirl of thoughts and feelings—the maybe, the what if, and the right now.

What she knew was that she had to know. She observed her hand remove the receiver from its hook, raised it to her ear.

"*Dime?*" Who's there?

"It's me." Colin's voice. The sound of his voice! Her hand trembled. Some little stubborn thing inside her gave way.

She raised her free hand to press the button, to open the door to the building. In a minute, she'd feel his arms around her again, feel his lips on hers. Her bed, still unmade, was two steps away.

With what felt like a tremendous exertion, Juliet drew her hand back away from the button. *I do not have to be the fool rushing in again.*

"I'll be right down!" The small victory elated her. She hung up the intercom, and took another moment to stand as she'd been standing, with her back to the door, surveying the little room that she'd been so excited to call her own for the summer. She pictured Colin waiting for her below in the Plaza de la Libertad.

And then, moving quickly, she removed the clothes that she'd had on all day. Stepped into her lightweight khaki pants. Applied deodorant. Pulled on her favorite scoop-necked gray t-shirt. Juliet glanced at herself in the mirror, and saw a healthy, smiling girl whose face was warm with sunshine and freedom. *Climb every mountain, right?* She laughed, tossed her hair, and headed out the door.

Her feet carried her down the stairs in rhythmic triplets, even as her mind attempted to pull her back. Colin's face lit up the moment he saw her reach the lobby.

She opened the heavy glass door, and stepped into his arms, felt his sweet mouth on hers. Time stopped. She melted into him.

And then, trying to observe with her coldly scientific mind's eye, she pulled away just a little. Thinking, *watch yourself.* Colin let her go.

"I've had such a productive afternoon!" he said. "Got back to making some progress with the lyrics. I was beginning to worry that I was going to lose my momentum."

Colin clasped her hand in his and they began to walk together. He went on talking animatedly about his experience of the creative process, how the interruption of flow states could sometimes result in interminable-seeming periods of glaciation.

"Everything can just freeze up. Something like an Ice Age can set in, so deep, so cold, I can't even imagine a thaw."

Juliet listened, and watched herself listening. And she felt some kind of cold creeping into her veins, as he tugged her along by the hand. Colin had his momentum. *Well, good for him. What about my momentum?* She had made a promise to herself. She was not going to just trade one guy in for another again.

"So, where do you think we're headed?" she interrupted. They stopped halfway across the Plaza Mayor.

"Good question!" Colin responded cheerily, facing her. "What do you feel like? Should we get a bite to eat?" He squeezed her hand and pulled, ready to head off in some direction.

"Maybe. But no. What I mean is…I was supposed to leave Salamanca tomorrow."

"I can be ready to leave, if you're ready to leave. Where do you want to go first?"

"Where do I want to go?"

"Sure! You choose. I'll go wherever you want, as long as it's not back to somewhere I've already been." Juliet felt Colin pulling at her hand again.

"So we're really going to go somewhere together?"

"Or we can stay here, if you'd like more time in Salamanca. I've got work I need to do, but I can do it pretty much anywhere."

"I've got work that I need to do, too, you know." Juliet pulled her hand away from his.

"Of course you do! I know. Great." Colin held his two hands out, with the palms facing down, unsure of what was happening. Then, he tilted his head, smiled questioningly, and added, "What work?"

"*What work?*" Juliet bristled, and her tone became a little bit strident as she asserted herself and her independence. "I told you. I'm starting a graduate program in systematic botany at Cornell University."

"Oh, that work. Sure, I remember. But…"

"But what?"

"But for now you're still on vacation, right?"

"I'm not here on vacation. I'm here to study Spanish."

"Of course. Sorry." Colin looked mystified. "But I thought you changed your flight to buy us some time."

"I don't know what I was thinking." Juliet uttered the words in a hollow voice. "I'm moving to Ithaca in seven weeks."

Colin shrugged. A look of disappointment darkened his features. "I guess I don't understand what you're saying."

"I guess I'm saying that I don't understand what we're doing together. You've got your momentum. And I've got mine. Just because we collided doesn't mean we have to get knocked off course."

"No. I can't let you knock me off course." Colin shook his head sadly. "And I sure wouldn't want to feel like I'm knocking you off course, either."

"Well, you're not."

"Good. That's not what I want to do."

They stood there in the Plaza Mayor, about two feet apart now, searching each other's faces, for something. Pedestrians and swallows moved around and past them. With her cold, scientific eye, Juliet observed the whole expanse of space and time moving in to fill the gap that already separated them from one another.

She saw herself moving ahead into the future alone, strong and steady. She saw herself remembering this warm, talented young man, and how she had been level-headed enough, this time, to pull her hand away and not get dragged off into something that wasn't her own.

"I'm sorry," she said. "We may as well just say goodbye right now."

Colin shrugged, burying his hands in his pockets. He was no stranger to loss.

"Goodbye, then."

"Goodbye."

Juliet lowered her eyes with an apologetic nod. *No good reason to postpone the inevitable.* Then she turned around and walked away from him slowly, heading back across the plaza toward her apartment. She had swept her deck clean. An immense stork circled the clock tower and clacked its beak before settling in its disheveled nest.

In a rapid rush of images, Juliet thought of Magda, and of Brad, and of the evening light on her grandmother's lake. She thought of her parents' proud smiles and her sister's faithful encouragement. She thought of her bright, imminent future. Scientific, observant, she registered the array of data which indicated that she was on the course that she had set for herself.

The bell in the tower clanged once, tolling the quarter hour. Juliet shook a bit of grit out of her sandal. Suddenly her thoughts turned to Santa Teresa and her interior castle of unfolding mysteries. *What was pulling at her?*

As they'd stood on the summit of the hill to the west of the city, earlier that very same day, Colin had picked up a shard of metal from an old can and had begun to dig carefully in the dry, rocky ground. When he stood up again, he'd handed her a few sprigs of thyme, roots largely intact. "I'll bet you can get this to grow anywhere," he'd said.

Mid-stride, Juliet felt all of the life and truth drain from her body. She had no science to explain it. There was no science to account for the horrible, tragic feeling with which she stopped in her tracks, and turned around to look back just once at the now empty spot where she'd showed her strength by saying goodbye to the most beautiful boy at the end of her summer in Spain.

And when she saw him still standing there watching her walk away—she had no science, either, that could explain the sparkling warm flood that rushed up through her legs from the paving stones beneath her feet, filling her eyes fast and full of tears.

In two seconds, they closed the distance that separated them. Pedestrians and swallows encircled them in a hallowed space.

"What was that?"

"I'm sorry! I'm really not ready to go anywhere away from you, now that I've found you. Not yet."

3

They had a month together in Spain. All these years later, while Juliet felt that she could still recollect every beat of their first twenty-four hours, her memories of their travels were discontinuous. Episodes and moments remained vivid and recurred in her consciousness unexpectedly over the years, triggered by sounds and smells and topics of conversation.

"An artist must catch every scrap of wind," Colin once told her, quoting Lawrence Durrell. Responding to her curious questions, he had tried to explain his creative principles, his artist's creed.

Not just scraps of wind but the day's last light caught in leaves, the geometric cross-cutting of shadows, certain habits of strands of hair that fell into her face, the tiniest muscle details of her expressions. She alternately flushed and glowed under the closeness of his scrutiny and was grateful that his observations, when he shared them out loud, more generally drew her attention to things outside herself. Things that she had never learned to notice before.

His awareness was acute beyond even her own, beyond anything she had experienced. She felt that there was nothing that escaped his attention—and yet, with a child's joy of discovery, he was constantly pointing out things right under their noses, even in the places that they almost made familiar together.

The soundscapes, as he called them, were what he found most absorbing, of course. At the most unexpected moments, he'd get this rapt look on his face—eyes wide, eyebrows lifted. Juliet learned to recognize when he was listening to something, and would try to hear it herself.

She came to think of his hearing as something like a dog's sense of smell, with power of discernment exponentially beyond her own. Sometimes she could pick up on some part of it: the rich peeling percussive sound of a car's tires on wet cobblestones as they crossed a narrow street during a cloudburst, the autumnal fluttering of crumpled cocktail napkins as the barman emptied his brimming dustpan into the wastebasket, and once, as her own hearing became more attuned, the rhythmic early morning intersection of milk being steamed and chairs being unstacked and scraped into place as two coworkers readied their bar for the day's business.

Colin had laughed with embarrassed delight when she'd interrupted his sudden absorption to hazard her guess at what had suddenly caught his attention.

"And imagine," he'd said with excitement. "It must sound exactly like that every single morning. Those two old fellows have obviously been working here for years, making this morning music together, without even knowing it or trying."

Colin went on to point out what she hadn't heard for herself, the other layers of the soundscape: the quiet whirring of the oscillating fan mounted on a corner shelf near the ceiling that ticked just so as it turned, the practiced rhythm of change-making as the barkeep dropped a customer's *cien pesetas* coin in his drawer, withdrew the two *duros* left after a *café con leche* and slapped them onto the bar with a guttural *que tenga buen día* and the customer's equally guttural *igualmente* rejoinder.

Colin's ears perked up at unexpected layers and juxtapositions. He had multi-dimensional hearing.

They laughed together again later in the day, when Colin had his guitar out and she recognized his musical representation of the morning. No one but her could ever have known its origins, but he'd unerringly replicated layers of interacting sounds that she lacked the vocabulary to describe.

"It's the only kind of prayer that comes naturally to me," he'd told her on another occasion. She'd been telling him about another one of her Spanish mystics, San Juan de la Cruz, and about his elaborate methodology for cultivating an ecstatic sensibility.

"I pay attention as closely as I can, I capture what I can capture, and sometimes, if I can, I build it into something that honors its distinct presence, whatever it is, some little shard of reality. Mostly, I am just bombarded by all these flying shards of reality that penetrate my awareness and fly right through me—like I'm a net with mesh too wide to hold anything. I play with whatever clings, but have to let most of it go without letting myself feel defeated by all the loss."

This creed, which Juliet felt and appreciated when Colin shared it with her, became more and more her own over the course of years of raising Gloria. She acutely felt herself to be a net with mesh too wide to hold anything, but sensitive enough to feel it all flying through her.

That was exactly what helped her get through the darkest times. That, and some life force in her of inexplicable origin which led to her stubborn refusal to be defeated by all the loss. She had an unfathomable depth of feeling for little things, the little shards of fragmented reality that opened up into whole worlds of feeling and memory as they cut through her. Like the smell of this otherworldly thyme that she crushed and bruised now, as she knelt in her Kansas garden, with fingers that were lovely still and that made her feel younger than her age.

As soon as Gloria was born, Juliet felt cut to the quick, and cut again, and again. She was sliced to ribbons every day by a kind of joy that she'd never imagined to be possible. It came flying at her from morning through the night. The smallest expressions on the baby's face. The creases in the tiny palms of her hands. Delight in new foods.

And the sounds, of course. Gloria spoke and hummed in symphonies and paragraphs of meaning and nuance long before she ever learned to form a word or sing a song. Juliet, with sharpened ears, learned every bit of her baby's language in the very moments of its invention.

Her flayed heart couldn't burst, there were no bounds to it at all anymore. All that was left of Juliet, that was not her daughter, was an intensity of gratitude and sorrow and an unshakeable feeling of kinship with every living thing.

Her intuitions had become like wings for her science. She had caught at every scrap of wind, every glimmer of light, every shade of soil, every bit of earthy wisdom from old farmers who shared things with her that no one else seemed to have ears to hear. She recognized it all for what it was, saw the whole cloak of reality in the bits and shards that flew through her. With the lightest touch, she helped it bear its most bounteous fruit.

From where she knelt in the corner of her garden, Juliet could hear Gloria's laughter. She was on the telephone, with some boy probably. There was a different one each week, it seemed. Juliet couldn't keep track of their names. They didn't date, didn't go steady.

She'd initially thought that Gloria's lack of romantic attachments was unique to her, perhaps a corollary of her focus on music, which sometimes seemed all-consuming. But then somewhere she'd read an article about it—it was a trend for Gloria's generation. They weren't pairing off and forming those strong bonds.

Juliet didn't quite understand the loose and short-lived alliances. Part of her suspected that maybe there was something sensible about it. She wondered about the trade-off. Less intensity, less premature commitment, and less heartbreak.

Even as she felt Gloria was sparing her from some teenage drama, Juliet couldn't help feeling motherly concern about a seemingly shallower depth of feeling. Maybe Gloria and her peers would be spared mid-life sentimentality about loves lost. But maybe they were missing out on laying important cornerstones of their identities that would help them bear the weight of all that life would throw at them later.

Would Juliet rather have been spared herself? Not for a minute.

Juliet felt her hands in the dry soil. She felt that her memories of a life lived with intensity of feeling formed her strongest attachment to the earth itself.

She dug her fingers into the ground and gripped it fiercely, relishing the roughness of it against her skin and under her nails. She'd be torn by it and broken up. To this dust she would return, her origin and her destination.

She didn't give way to the sudden impulse to smear it, inscribe it, on her teary face. But she marveled at the pagan strength of the urge.

Juliet could barely remember the vague abstraction of what she had thought was her love for that childhood fiancé. She'd been so detached and unfeeling. The entire engagement was Juliet playing a role in a pretty story. They were hometown sweethearts, so appropriate, so happy, so pre-programmed. They were cardboard cut-out characters, with not an iota of abandon or earthy lust for life.

She shuddered now at the thought of how close she'd come to sleepwalking her way into a magazine-display marriage. And shuddered again, deliciously, when she remembered that early morning abandoning of all form and convention and script in the Plaza de la Libertad.

Juliet inhaled deeply, and felt the cleansing stream of her own tears. She could smell the shards of fleeting reality that still clung to the strands of her net: sweat and tobacco and *chocolate*.

They took buses and trains. They hitchhiked to get to places that could only be reached by car. Everything they saw, in all weather, was heightened and warmed by the balmy conditions they created for themselves.

A bickering couple stopped to pick them up somewhere in the Picos de Europa. While the driver and his wife asked them stiffly polite questions and otherwise sat in stony cold silence, Colin and Juliet clung to each other's hands in the back seat and looked out the windows at the impenetrable gray banks of clouds that shed more and more moisture as they curved and wound upward on a narrow mountain road. Juliet was making herself count the weeks that remained of her summer, with undisclosed dread. At the summit, they stopped in cold rain, thanked their gloomy drivers, and rushed into the shelter of a restaurant in a stone hut that looked as if it had been there since the dawn of time.

Their damp faces soon glowed in the warmth of the giant wood fire. They ate deep bowls of strongly-flavored *fabada asturiana*. They drank bottles of the bittersweet hard cider that they took turns decanting, and laughed at their efforts to imitate the dexterity of the other patrons, who poured the lightly carbonated golden fluid in smooth streams from a full arm's length.

The rain had stopped when they stepped outside, both of them full of the heavy stew and a little bit tipsy. They walked, half stumbling, down a grassy slope until they felt all alone and invisible in the thick fog that rang and clanked with the gentle tones of sheep bells.

Colin produced a tarp from his backpack, and made a little nest of garments for them on the soft ground. They lay down together, with intertwined legs and soft kisses, and fell asleep in each other's arms.

When they awoke, every scrap of fog had vanished. They lay there in bright sunshine under an unblemished blue sky that was doubled in brilliance by the perfect mountain lake just a few yards farther down the slope. For a few minutes, Juliet felt some relief from the terrible sensation of the shortness of time which had been oppressing her.

In Covadonga they visited the shrine and the caves and the hermitage. Juliet shared what she knew about Pelayo and the victory over the Moors that marked the beginning of the *Reconquista*. The sight of Colin's face, looking at her with rapt interest, with the huge mouth of the cave in the background, always stuck with her.

"*Pelayo de Covadonga,*" he shouted, testing an echo against the stony mountainside. Drawing stares. Not caring.

"*Covadonga!*" He shouted again.

He'd loved the sound of the word. That night, in their tiny room, while Juliet dozed off after their lovemaking, he'd sat by the window that opened onto the narrow, iron-railed balcony with his guitar and toyed with lyrics and sound. Juliet thought she could hear the fog-bound clanking of sheep bells.

"Covadonga, my love." He sang softly, so as not to disturb her, or maybe to keep to himself the imperfections of work in progress. "Covadonga, my love, bright mountain pool, *sueño con la reconquista de tu cuerpo.*"

As Juliet remembered it, they had made love every day. Sometimes more than once, morning and night, or afternoon. She hadn't previously known herself to be such a creature of the flesh. She could hardly recognize herself in the intensity of her desire. Closeness to him was more urgent than any hunger for food or thirst for drink.

In some shop, somewhere along the way, they'd picked up a collection of short stories by Dylan Thomas. The morning after reading "A Visit to Grandpa's" they took a bumpy, curvy bus ride along the coast. They both clutched the backs of the seats in front of them just to stay in their seats.

"Whoa there, my beauties," Colin cried, citing the story, and they laughed until they gasped for breath.

"Gee-up! Gee-up!" he said, every time they seemed to be about to recover their composure—and the laughter would start all over again.

The bus wasn't crowded. There was a handful of old folks on board, men and women. Their raucous and uncontrollable laughter drew a few scowls of disapproval—and at least one sparsely-toothed smile that Juliet could still see, as she remembered.

She remembered the intensity of her wanting during that bus trip as vividly as she remembered the intensity of their laughter. As the bus bounced and swayed, as they jostled against each other, Juliet felt Colin's corduroy thigh pressing against hers—and just wanted his body so completely, so intensely that she felt herself flushing with a kind of awe. The incoherence of it merged indistinguishably with the wild laughter that kept shaking its way up from deep inside.

She wanted to smash and break against him like the Cantabrian waves that smashed against the dark rocks down below the narrow road. She freed a hand from its grip on the seat back, and gripped his thigh instead.

By the time they finally made it behind a closed door, the wanting had surged and subsided a dozen times over the course of the day. On the bus, on the beach, when he wrote out lyrics for her in the sand that the sea wiped away as she read them. The wanting surged in sudden swells, in sidelong glances, in little bursts of conversation and understandings, in touchings, and emphatic grasping, and embraces. When he slipped his arm around her tummy from behind and rested his chin on her shoulder, just to better see what she was seeing.

In San Sebastian they'd eaten like neither of them had ever eaten anywhere before. They stayed in their room until early afternoon, and then made their way from bar to bar—where the array of *pintxos* dazzled and beckoned them onward until they were stuffed silly. They walked along the waterfront, holding hands, talking.

Juliet was struggling with herself. Any day now, she was going to have to book her flight home. She was anxious that she'd already put it off for too long. Her future at Cornell was coming on fast.

"This is love, right?"

"Let's see…" Colin held up a hand to count on his fingers. "You make everything double for me. That old looking and waiting feeling that I've had for as long as I can remember? Gone without a trace. Instead of thinking about what I want to do, I wake up every morning wondering what you might want to do. My life before you feels now, in memory, like half a life, a shadow. Looking forward…well, I don't see the way forward yet, but know that a future without you in it feels like a cold, black pit. So…yeah. This is love, I'm pretty sure."

Juliet hugged him. Then whispered in his ear.

"Or maybe you just want to get all of my clothes off of me again."

"It's *and*, not *or*. And there's no *maybe*."

They walked a stretch of the famous pilgrims' way near Santiago de Compostela. For so many of the steps they took together, Juliet experienced the profoundest contentment she'd ever known. She was just there beside her summer love, moving slowly through the rush of time. At other moments, as her clock counted down relentlessly, she felt crushed and bruised and out of her mind. She didn't know, she was afraid to ask, how Colin's clock was running.

One night, there was no room for them at the only inn within miles. It was a warm night and, with little discussion, they just made themselves as comfortable as they could with their limited and improvised equipment, and lay down under the starry sky in an open field.

"All that space. All that silence between the stars."

"I wish I knew more of their names."

"There's so many tonight, I can't even find the few that I do know."

"I don't think I've ever seen the Milky Way shine so brightly."

"We are so small."

"And sometimes so big on the inside."

"We are made of the same stuff as the stars."

"Living stardust. Twinkles in time."

"Walking, talking."

"Finding each other, in all that space and time."

"Let's hold on tight."

"I'm holding on."

As soon as they entered the outskirts of the ancient city, Juliet saw a *locutorio*. She couldn't postpone booking her return for more than another day or two. In some quiet agony, she went inside and placed a call to her graduate department. She didn't commit herself to making any kind of a decision. She just had to ask the question that had taken form in her mind along the *camino*. What if?

She returned to the street just a very few minutes later with her state of mind dramatically altered, though not for the better. Deferring her start of the program would be a routine matter, if that's what she decided she needed to do. People did it all the time, she'd been told. She shrugged her shoulders into the straps of her backpack, and felt the heavy weight of her freedom as she walked beside Colin toward the terminus of their brief pilgrimage.

In the old cathedral, they watched the endless line of pilgrims awaiting their turn to kneel at the foot of the statue of the saint.

"So much faith." Juliet said, on the verge of something.

"So much desperate and devoted hope—such hunger for forgiveness, understanding, meaning. Such love and gratitude. What stardust does when it finds itself with legs and hearts."

He got it, better than she did. And he made a better effort at saying it. She squeezed his hand and looked at him as he gazed upwards at the soaring heights of stone. *Who am I fooling?* She thought, shaking her head at herself. She let go, finally, right then, of the stubborn and false part of herself that had been holding out in indecision.

They checked themselves into a comfortable *pensión* a block away from the cathedral plaza. While Colin showered, Juliet went out and called her department again. She could wait to begin her degree program. She could not pretend for another minute to be anything like ready to fly away from Colin.

They tried turning southward from the coast after Santiago, but only made it as far as León before the austerity of the plains and their hardened people turned them northward again. It barely took them an exchange of glances over morning coffee to agree to reverse their direction. Juliet's undivided heart felt lighter in her chest than it had ever felt before.

Back in Asturias, they took their time again, walking on beaches and high grassy bluffs over the sea. They spent rainy afternoons in ramshackle *sidrerías*. By now they'd both acquired some expertise at decanting the bittersweet golden cider in shimmering streams. They ate *queso de cabrales* until they lost their appetite for it.

After the first few days of their travels together, Colin had let his performance routine go. He had enough money so that there was no urgency. He turned inward—preferring to spend long quiet evenings in the room with Juliet. While she dozed off, he'd get out his guitar and notebook and worked.

Falling asleep to his music in the making was the memory that knit all the rest of the memories together, and made one hotel room blend irrecoverably into the next. Always, as she remembered it, Colin sat between the bed and the window. He sat in profile to her, his guitar on his knee, and his notebook on the edge of the bed. He sang bits of lyrics in a low, sweet voice—not wanting to disturb her sleep, and not yet ready to share.

Juliet caught snatches of things that stuck with her. There was a bright trumpet on a dusky river. Coffee and cream and spent pencil dreams. Walking uphill backwards to make it feel like going down. Hours at night that flew faster than day. High above the diamond city, a secret rite of superheroes. Forget all peril, wrap us up in all our wings and fall.

One night, instead of playing and writing, Colin just stood on the balcony for a long time gazing out at the immense full moon that they'd been marveling at ever since it rose above the dark rim of the sea. Juliet had thought she was tired, and had even fallen asleep for awhile. But without the lullaby sound of his voice and strings—she'd gotten so accustomed to it—she lay there awake watching him and thinking about joining him outside.

He turned and saw her eyes open, shining in the silvery moonlight. "You're awake."

"I guess I miss my sweet lullaby serenading."

"I'm sorry. I can play something for you."

"That's okay. You're not in the mood tonight?"

"I think I'm ready to go back. I started something that I think I'm ready to finish."

Suddenly, Juliet felt exposed and foolish, and her heart sank like lead. She'd finally committed herself—and hadn't secured a commitment in return. But Colin, not noticing her distress, explained to her about Kassabian and how he had left the country and suspended his recording contract. He apologized for not having told her all about it before.

"I guess I have issues about not wanting to count any chickens before they're hatched."

"Seems like maybe you've got issues about letting on that you're sitting on some important eggs."

"I don't want to go back. I want to cross the Pyrenees with you and hitchhike to Italy, to the Cinque Terre, to Paestum, like we've been saying. But I'm torn. I've got this chance to make a record."

Juliet sat up. "I'll go with you."

"Simple as that?"

"I'm your perfect traveling companion, remember?"

4

On her knees, in her garden, Juliet sat back on her heels and listened to the familiar strains of *Sunshine & Thyme*, and marveled at the richness of her daughter's voice. Romeo's Beat had been another one of the musical marvels of the late eighties. Colin had named the band because of her, of course. The maps on the album cover that he had designed showed some of the territory that they had traveled, and still hoped to travel, together.

He was her Romeo, and this was his beat. The title track, *Highest Law*, which never got as much radio play as the rest of the album, proclaimed the *'round the world revolution, that made love the highest law in every land*.

Sunshine & Thyme was the first hit and had been on the airwaves continuously since its first release. Juliet had heard it so often over the years that it had become just a turbulent undercurrent in the background of her life. Gloria's voice brought it all roiling to the surface again.

She had long ago stopped wishing she could forget the first time she'd heard it on the car radio. Juliet had been all alone, and too distracted to listen. The lyrics were unfamiliar to her. Colin had produced and recorded that particular track with all kinds of romantic secrecy.

"It's a dedication," he'd told her.

Lyrical fragments of it were familiar to her from those late night hotel rooms, and had become interwoven with her dreams, forgotten and remembered. The whole album was for her. This song was the special surprise that he'd withheld, wanting her to hear it live for the first time on the first night of the Romeo's Beat *Highest Law* tour.

The plan was that they would spend two months in LA—time enough for Colin and the band to get their act back together and make their recording. Then, he and Juliet would fly back to Europe and pick up where they had left off. They would have another six weeks or so of travel together before the next start date for Juliet's graduate program.

Though every intervening week was already accounted for, the looming separation felt remote. And facing it head on together made it feel not so terrible, like something that they would be ready to take in stride when the time came. They understood that there would be distance, but agreed that it would not divide them. But within a few weeks of their arrival in California, it became clear that their plans were going to change again.

They had sublet a little house in Hollywood from a friend of Colin's sister. It was tiny and cluttered with pottery and ceramics, and had an overgrown vegetable garden and a genuine Juan Gris on an otherwise unadorned living room wall. It also had a car that they could use, a Toyota Corona station wagon with a manual transmission and faux wood side panels. From the driveway they could see the middle of the Hollywood sign. Melrose and the Paramount studios were within walking distance. They were amazed by the number of times they got home at night and looked up through the city sky at stars through clouds. But, other than to stumble in at ridiculous hours and crash on the double mattress in the middle of the bedroom floor, they didn't spend much time there.

The recording process, as Colin had hardly realized, and as they both quickly learned, was all-absorbing. Ordinary time had no meaning there. Colin was apologetic—torn between his desire to do his best work, and his desire to be with Juliet, intimate and private. But Juliet really didn't mind at all. She was fascinated by the creative process, the collaboration, the technology, the tense atmosphere of heightened excitement when the producer brought other representatives from the label, from the industry, from the press, into the studio.

She made herself as useful as she could, wholly caught up in it. It became something that they were doing together.

"Am I your groupie? Or your roadie?" She'd teased as they undressed for bed at four in the morning.

"You're my muse," he'd said, reaching for her.

"Right now, I'm your grody."

They'd laughed then, and showered together, before curling up in each other's naked arms. Too tired to make love, and too happy to care.

Juliet had been right there when Kassabian came in and announced to the band between takes that he was in the process of booking them for a months-long album release tour in small- to mid-size venues in sixteen different cities. They'd be headlining in some small clubs and on some campuses. In the larger venues, they'd be opening for some of the major artists on the label.

Colin and Juliet had looked at each other, seeing their plans for a return to Europe vanish. She could see in his look how conflicted he was feeling, how ready he was to voice some protest. She just shook her head, and shrugged, and smiled. They were in it together, and it was as great an adventure, or greater, as they could have anywhere.

5

Juliet didn't spend all of her time in the studio. As interesting as it was, and as much as she wanted to be near Colin at all hours, after the first few weeks she began to feel like she wasn't herself anymore. Confined inside the studio for hours and hours at a stretch, time took on characteristics that were unfamiliar to her. They'd finally step out onto the sidewalk into blazing sunshine, when Juliet expected it to be the middle of the night. The band got hungry and ordered fried chicken and barbecue at seven in the morning. And then everybody would forget about food completely for what felt like days. There was some focused back and forth about a tiny little detail, getting a car horn to sound at just the right time, with just the right tone, for just the right amount of time.

Juliet looked up at the hands on the numberless clock on the wall from where she sat slumped in a brown leather beanbag chair. Through bleary eyes, she couldn't be sure if she was reading the time correctly, or whether four hours had passed since they'd started working out the problem of the car horn. Colin noticed.

"You're drooping."

"I'm wilting a little, maybe." Her bright voice had gone flat.

"It's the car horn, isn't it? I knew it."

Juliet laughed. But weakly. She wasn't sure what it was.

"You need to get outside."

"When we're done here."

"No. It's not healthy for you. You need sunshine and greenery."

"Maybe I could take a little walk."

"Out you go!" Colin helped her up out of the beanbag, and hugged her tight. Then he walked her to the door. "Sunshine. Greenery. You know where to find me. We've got a ways to go yet."

Colin was right. Given her natural affinity for growing things, and for the light and air that were essential to all such growth, and unaccustomed to spending such long periods of time shut up in windowless studios, Juliet's circadian rhythms had gotten out of whack.

She spent an afternoon wandering aimlessly around their Hollywood neighborhood. She got a good night's sleep, during the night time, and felt much more like herself the next morning.

Finding that she had more time to herself than she had expected, Juliet began to orient herself to the botanical diversity and resources of the region. Just walking around their neighborhood, her eyes were agog at the plant life of southern California. Succulents, uninterrupted by winter or any shortage of water, were immense and thriving beyond anything she'd ever seen before. Entire houses were covered in bougainvillea. Spindly palm trees swayed gently, their fronds reflecting glints of sunlight at tremendous heights.

She had planted her little cutting of thyme from the Salamanca hillside in a ceramic pot on their cement stoop the day after they'd taken possession of the rented house. Now, she started to surround it with little pots of all shapes and sizes, cultivating little snips of things that she gathered surreptitiously during her walks. Life forms that she had never seen before took root and began to thrive under her care. She learned their Latin names, and their origins. So few of them were endemic. This whole desert flood plain, it turned out, had been planted by generations of nameless and forgotten gardeners.

As she began to assert herself amongst the vegetables growing in the small backyard, she wondered about the person who'd first prepared the beds of soil and built the boxes around them. The heavy beams of wood were weathered but still sturdy, and held together with rusted iron bolts. The three beds were positioned perfectly to maximize sun exposure from one end of the day to the other. Whoever it was had watched carefully, to see how the shadows from surrounding houses, fences, and trees fell as the earth rotated.

Juliet could see, from the intermingled foliage and unharvested produce, that the garden had received no attention for a season or more. People start gardens, she reflected, with no thought of what becomes of them or of how they may evolve when left untended. She identified the true perennials and cleared away all of the annuals that had held on due to the winterless climate, until the rich, dark soil separating the plants appeared, making the beds look neat and tidy.

While Colin's days and nights ran together irregularly, as he and his band dedicated themselves to their art with complete absorption, Juliet spent long days exploring the Huntington Gardens in San Marino. Leveraging her acceptance letter from Cornell, she sought and obtained permission to review manuscripts held in the library's famous rare books collection.

Juliet marveled at the careful illustrations and precise observations, the emerging standardization of nomenclature, and the dogged pursuit of understanding of growth and cell structure. She felt that she had found close friends, though she'd never met them, and they'd all died long ago.

"Tucked away in that library, I'm surrounded by more of my people than I've met over the course of my entire life. Only, they're all dead!"

"Huh." Colin tilted his head sideways at her.

It must have been two in the afternoon, and he was behaving exactly as if it were two in the morning. Standing there wearing a faded blue t-shirt, and nothing else. About to collapse into the mattress on the floor.

"It's like…the stuff they cared about is the same stuff I care about, only I couldn't really have said so, if I hadn't realized it while sitting there with them. They were telling each other things, and they're talking to me, too. But I can't talk back, because they're all dead."

Juliet was pretty sure that she was only talking to herself even now. Colin was plainly within instants of unconsciousness. For her, it was just getting to be the hour when she would make herself a cup of tea and get out her notebook and pen, and get some of what she had observed down on paper.

The earliest botanical illustrators had been close, but not perfect, observers. After capturing a certain amount of detail, they couldn't really see past their own powerful imaginations.

They looked, and they saw. But then, when trying to depict or describe what they saw, they only went so far, and then they just made up all the rest by themselves. They imposed a symmetry. Or something.

Juliet wanted to show them that, if they'd only kept looking, they could've seen it, too. It had always all been there. They just didn't have the attention span.

Or maybe they just couldn't believe what they were seeing. Life was so strikingly irregular at the cellular level, as if only half sketched in by a Creator who trusted in life's own energy to fill in the finest details. She could see them beginning to come to terms with it during the late sixteenth century.

"I think you can talk back."

"What?" For a second, she thought Colin was talking in his sleep.

"Just because they're dead, it doesn't mean that you can't talk back."

"Uh, sure. I mean, I know I can talk all I want."

"No, really. You can be part of the conversation. You are part of the conversation. You don't even know what an important part of the conversation you may be."

Colin was flat on his back now, his head on the pillow. Juliet pulled the sheet and beige flannel blanket up to his neck, half kneeling on the ground beside the mattress. She'd found the blanket on a high shelf in the cupboard in the middle of their second night when, with all the windows open to the summer air, she'd been surprised awake by the unexpected chill.

116

She pressed her lips to his forehead. She closed her eyes and inhaled the warm smell of his scalp through his tousled hair.

"Seriously, though," he continued, with his eyes closed. "You hear them talking to you. You write in response and it's like you're talking right back at them. Then, a hundred, two hundred years from now, you're all talking to each other and to someone who's not even alive right now. And that someone doesn't even realize that you were talking to the dead. To that someone, you're all the same amount of dead. And you're all still talking to each other, and to the living. And to people who haven't even been born yet."

Now it was Juliet's turn to tilt her head sideways. But Colin was snoring before she could formulate a next thought.

He got up to go back to the studio while she was asleep, and for a couple of days their schedules were completely at odds. They took turns gazing at each other's sleeping forms.

Some days later, they were sitting side by side on the sand in Malibu watching small, perfect waves curl and then crash onto the shore. Colin surprised her by remembering the strange conversation they'd had while he was falling asleep.

He held her hand and in a steady voice told her about the death of his parents. First his mother and then, right after, his father. He said that he was sorry, that he should have told her before now.

Stricken by this revelation, Juliet had no words. She just clung to his hand tenderly, taking shallow breaths and feeling tears welling in her eyes.

He talked about his parents often, and so lovingly, with such admiration for their happy marriage. He had just left out the fact that he was mourning their loss. He hadn't felt ready to share that heaviness, or to introduce that sorrow into the joy they were finding together.

"But this is what I meant the other night by talking back to the dead," he explained. "I talk to them all the time. I wouldn't be able to bear it otherwise. I couldn't be me without talking to them. And, I can still hear their voices. Things they said play on and on inside me, and sometimes it's like I'm hearing them for the first time just because of where I am now. Or something happens, and I think of something they said that I had forgotten."

"They're alive inside you."

"That's right. And your historical botanists are alive inside you. Like my musician heroes are alive inside me."

"And if we talk back, add our voices…"

"We'll be part of something that is so much bigger, that just doesn't stop at death."

6

During her waking hours, Juliet buried herself in the library, writing and drawing. Notes became paragraphs and then pages with full-colored figures as she grew more and more comfortable talking back to her dead people, joining herself to their quiet but passionate company. She picked up where they had left off, completed thoughts and observations with her own careful illustrations, and carried them until she felt that she was pushing at her own limits.

She discovered that she was both more and less than she had ever expected. Not just in her studies and work, but in the magical dust that swirled in beams of light around her and Colin. She could stretch all the way out toward remotest frontiers of perception, and there see how little of that reach was hers alone.

The intensity of their complete around the clock immersion in each other's company while they were in Spain, as recent as that was, had, with terrible speed, become part of the past. They both looked back with fond longing as it receded. They couldn't rewind time.

Their feelings for each other only grew. They hungered for more time together and found comfort in a quiet sense of certainty that, now that they had begun to grow together, intertwined, it was irreversible.

They so quickly got to a place where they could see it going on that way for the rest of their lives. Colin had his thing, and Juliet had hers. And though they were separate things, and they knew that they were going to have to endure some separations, they were wholly wrapped up in each other.

There were a few interruptions in Colin's intense recording schedule, when he and his band had to surrender the recording studio to other artists with pressing deadlines of their own. At the beginning of one of these anticipated breaks, Colin returned to the little house late in the afternoon and found Juliet waiting for him excitedly. She had packed for both of them. Colin saw the two compact duffel bags on the floor as soon as he stepped through the door.

"What's up?"

"We're going on an adventure."

"Where to?"

"Twenty six miles across the sea."

"Santa Catalina?"

Juliet beamed, and held up the bikini that she was about to stuff in her bag.

They held hands throughout the long drive south across L.A. to Long Beach Harbor. They didn't say much, but just took turns squeezing each other's hands to point things out along the road. Colin felt the old excitement of travel rising inside him like a spring tide.

Again and again, he turned to look at his partner, appreciating every little detail of her. The shape of her nose, the soft, warm glow in her cheek, the curve of her eyebrows, the steady lift at the corner of her lips that pressed and held in shape the perfect dimple. He wanted to be able to see all of her with his eyes closed, always. But no image he formed in his mind, however beloved and close to true, could ever replicate the vibrant reality of her presence.

During the boat ride across the channel, they stood on deck with their arms on the rail gazing at the sea and at the long mountain of an island that acquired more and more color as they drew closer. The air and the depths of the water grew clearer and clearer as the great city receded. They cried out at the same time when they saw flying fish. And then there were dolphins racing along beside the boat, and a raft of sea lions.

For two days of hiking and swimming in perfect weather, they didn't have to share each other with anyone or anything. Juliet found and sketched three of the six plant species that grow on the island and nowhere else: St. Catherine's lace, Santa Catalina bedstraw, and, after a long trek to Wild Boar Gully, the Catalina mahogany, the rarest tree in North America.

They visited the little island history museum and read about the first European visitor, Juan Rodríguez Cabrillo, and about Sebastián Vizcaíno, who rediscovered the island on the eve of St. Catherine's day and named it in her honor.

"I don't know why it took me so long to realize...we're still in Spain!" Colin marveled, standing before an early map of the California coast.

"St. Catherine said, *the path to heaven lies through heaven and all the way to heaven is heaven,*" Juliet said with delight, reading from a little hagiography that she'd pulled from the bookstore shelf.

Colin's sister Clara flew down from the Bay Area to stay with them for a couple of days. On the way to Burbank airport to pick her up, Juliet was nervous.

"What if she doesn't like me?"

"I guess I'd have to stop liking you immediately. Probably leave you in baggage claim."

Juliet swatted his leg. They both laughed. She still felt a little nervous.

Though she'd never seen her before, Juliet recognized Clara the instant she came out of the jetway into the arrivals lounge. The resemblance was slight, as Colin had warned, but the broad smile on her face unmistakably revealed her to be his sister. Colin and Clara hugged. Then Clara turned to Juliet.

"So. You're the groupie."

Juliet opened her mouth. But Clara didn't wait for her to splutter.

"I've always wanted a sister," she said, pulling her into a laughing embrace.

They spent two days exploring L.A. neighborhoods. They drove around Boyle Heights looking at the murals painted by Chicano artists and shared an enormous burrito at El Tepeyac. Having discovered that they were all *Blade Runner* fans, they visited the Bradbury Building downtown. Then they emerged from the Grand Central Market with armloads of edibles and spent the most important part of the visit in the kitchen.

Clara and Colin cooked together, as they had done all their lives. A dexterous and light-hearted team, they made their grandmother's recipes, that their father had taught them, and some new recipes of their own, inspired by what they'd brought home from the market. Juliet sat on a stool, doing whatever odd jobs she was assigned, glowing in the warmth they were making together. Listening and asking questions, she drew out their details, and sometimes hazarded understandings of things that hadn't fully made sense to them.

There were *empanadas*, spaghetti with a sauce that had pine nuts, and a huge pot of special navy beans. As they cooked, they talked and laughed. Telling stories about their childhood and their parents, remembering their dead, they drew Juliet inside a family that spanned generations of time. When they returned Clara to the airport, Juliet felt acutely that the two siblings living at such a distance was a temporary wrong that had to be remedied somehow.

"See?" Clara said, as they hugged goodbye. "Sisters!"

"Sisters," Juliet confirmed, understanding as never before that we make, and find, and are not only born into, our families.

The next time there was a significant break in Colin's schedule, they visited the old Spanish mission and botanic garden at Santa Barbara. On another quick adventure, they got up before dawn and went to the mission at San Juan Capistrano. Besides pursuing the continuity of their Spanish experience, Juliet wanted to see the largest specimen of *Schinus molle*, the California pepper tree.

When there was less time to spare, they snuck away at all hours to the beach and pier in Santa Monica. The steady beating of the Pacific waves on the shore created a sense of timelessness for them.

One day, in late afternoon, they made their way to Olvera Street and were disappointed by the kitschy tourist shops that almost completely obscured any traces of the early architecture. But while there, they were thrilled to learn that L.A., the great city with the shortest name, had once had one of the longest: *el Pueblo de Nuestra Señora la Reina de los Ángeles sobre el Rio Porciúncula.*

Juliet bought a large topographical map of the greater LA area and hung it on the wall. One night, late, Colin stood in front of it in just his underwear and chanted Spanish place names. San Gabriel, San Fernando, San Rafael, Figueroa, Colorado, Palos Verdes, La Brea, La Cienega, Los Feliz, La Tijera, Sepulveda, La Mirada, Mar Vista, Pico Rivera, El Monte, El Molino, Cerritos, Redondo Beach, Playa del Rey, Arroyo Seco. Juliet was in bed, but awake. She watched and listened with a sleepy smile on her face as he experimented with rhythms and danced in place.

She was never sure who initiated it, but somehow they had both taken to exclaiming "Santa Monica, Santa Catalina!" in surprise or exasperation. It became their shared mantra or prayer. When one began it, the other completed it.

Years later, she still said it now and then, both halves, always with a little bittersweet pang in her heart for the early days of the adventure that they had set out on together. Eventually, after much hunting around, she acquired a little icon of each saint. She kept them side by side on a little table by the front door, a kind of multi-layered blessing and remembrance on the way in and out of the house.

7

The week before Romeo's Beat was scheduled to go on the road, Juliet flew home to Kansas City to spend a few days with her family. She and her father had the same birthday, and they'd never been apart for the celebration. The plan was that she was going to fly to Seattle on the morning after the birthday, to be there for the first night of the tour.

She hadn't been home since she'd left for Spain. She'd wanted to try and bring them all up to speed. She knew that she wasn't ready to share all of the truth. She wasn't altogether in touch with the whole truth of it herself, and didn't even fully understand that she would have the whole rest of her life for that.

Even with regard to the most immediate, pressing future, she felt more than a little bit hopeless at the prospect of trying to get them to understand. She had left three and a half months ago for a summer Spanish language program, and now had postponed her graduate school plans, and was on the verge of spending weeks on end touring around the country with a busload full of musicians.

Her family defied her expectations by taking it all in stride with a minimum of drama. No more Brad? A shrug of their shoulders. A musician she'd met in Spain? Unplanned weeks in a recording studio in LA? Love, as she'd never experienced before, and couldn't articulate now? A road trip in a bus across multiple states?

Their reaction was just as far as could be from what she had expected. If anything, their little smiles, and what might even have been little elbow nudges, made it look like they were excited to hear about it.

Who were these people? She looked at them like she'd never seen them before. A gray-headed pair sitting side by side on the well-worn gingham sofa where she'd experienced most of her life's drama, and vicarious drama. So many old movies! So much emotion built up around the simplest failures to communicate directly the most urgent truths.

Her mom and dad were to her so much more well-worn, and comfortable, and better known than any mute piece of furniture. They looked like they were part of each other. She acutely felt herself, and her sister, to be the fruit of the tree that they formed between them.

They wanted to hear about her writing and her drawing and her time in the library. They asked for more details about her travels through the north of Spain. Their laughter and curiosity made her eyes brim with heavy tears. But she didn't let them see. Nor did she let them hear the thickness in her throat which made it nearly impossible to speak. Juliet felt weirdly old, and incredibly relieved.

There was so much more to tell: the still microscopic detail that was going to make all the difference in all their lives. But she wasn't ready to tell it. She would have fallen apart completely.

And it was not for them to hear first, in any case. She understood that, with some grave depth of unanticipated understanding. She felt terrible, and at the same time, she felt herself to be uplifted on some kind of immense wave of unconditional love.

To cap things off, her parents bought her sister a plane ticket, as a birthday present for Juliet, so that they could go to Seattle together for the first two Romeo's Beat shows.

On Friday afternoon, the day before her birthday, Juliet was stopped at a red light on her way home from the mall. She was obsessing, as she had been for weeks, about the microscopic detail that was still her secret, about how Colin was going to take the news, and about how, exactly, she was going to tell him.

She couldn't believe her ears when the radio announcer said that the next song, *Sunshine & Thyme*, was from a soon-to-be-released album by a new band called Romeo's Beat. The song was being played as a special tribute.

It didn't make any sense. Colin would have told her, so that she'd be sure not to miss it. They'd just spoken on the phone that morning.

Then the announcer read out the dedication. "*For Juliet, my bounty is as boundless as the Cantabrian sea, My love as deep; the more I give to thee, the more I have, for both are infinite.*"

"After a terrible bus accident in northern Oregon," the announcer continued. "Four young men, all members of the new band Romeo's Beat, were pronounced dead at the scene. Colin Hogan, 23, was the band's songwriter, guitarist, and lead vocalist. Jim Fuller, 21, was the bass player. Gene Mueller, 23, played the drums. Fernando Montes, 25, was the band's keyboardist. They were on their way to Seattle for the opening performance of the promotional tour for their soon-to-be-released album, *Highest Law.* Here, then, for the first time but not, we're very sure, for the last, is *Sunshine & Thyme* by Romeo's Beat."

And that, was that. The light turned green. The car waiting behind her had to honk twice to get Juliet to move through the intersection. Somehow, she managed to drive herself the rest of the way home. She carried her packages inside and put them down on the table. Then she turned and, with an animal moan, collapsed into her mother's arms.

CODA

Over the years, Juliet had given a lot of thought to the notion that only the good die young. She had tried a million ways not to remember Colin as wholly good. She had tried to reframe the love they'd shared as something less than love, something juvenile, something half-baked. There had to be a crack in there somewhere.

Diminishing their love was a natural-enough impulse as she washed back and forth like flotsam through the stages of grief that seized her, let her go, and then, unpredictably, returned to seize her again. But it was only when she acknowledged that any diminishment of what she'd felt, what they'd shared, was a lie that she felt any strength inside her.

For a terribly short time, as a very young woman, she had experienced a perfect love. There was nothing illusory about it, and nothing that fell short. With Colin, she had learned about the fusion-power of the present moment, how by turning her attention to what passed before her and by letting herself go, she could allow everything to light up in bright color. And then she had experienced utter loss. She'd lost her bearings completely and for a long time she drifted.

Dying young, she'd finally decided, was the only imperfection. Colin had been a perfect gift to her. Given and taken away before she was twenty-four.

Live long enough and the shortcomings have time to make themselves apparent, especially through our fractured lenses. Love long enough and the challenges of loving someone perfectly, due to one's own imperfections if nothing else, will make itself known. Juliet didn't doubt that it would have been different if Colin had not died in that accident.

But she did not live in the conditional perfect tense. Truth is confined and constrained by the singularity of time. Colin didn't have time to show her his shortcomings. She'd only had time to love him easily, perfectly, irresistibly.

She often thought of San Martín and his torn cloak. What she had shared with Colin, so briefly, had been no half measure. During their time together there had been no need for grace to compensate them for any shortfalls. And in those final weeks before the bus accident, by some great mystery or fluke of the universe, Juliet had the grace she would ultimately depend upon to recover her life and strength growing in her womb.

At first, mourning shrouded her completely, like a black dress that had gotten stuck over her head. She could not see out, and was unapproachable. But even as she crumpled into herself in loneliness and devastation, the life they had created together was surging inside her.

Sharply mindful of their conversations, Juliet talked almost incessantly to her own beloved dead, at first in anxious, fearful lamentations. She reproached herself bitterly for having withheld the news of her pregnancy from him, telling herself that she had denied him what might have provided some instant of consolation at the end.

At the same time, she also talked to the tiny human that was growing inside her. There was a love story to tell, about a father who could only be known through stories. It had to be told to Gloria. She named her nearly right away, as she lay inconsolable in her parents' house, and began mumbling little prayers for wisdom and guidance, her hands clutching the belly that roiled while all the rest of her felt like dead earth.

128

Romeo's Beat was omnipresent during those long months. First, *Sunshine & Thyme*, then track after track, as the uniquely fresh and somehow nostalgic sound conspired with the tragic death of the artist to make *Highest Law* the top-selling and Grammy-winning album of the year.

Juliet couldn't bear to listen. She had no appetite for music, and never turned on the radio. But it was inescapable. She heard Colin's disembodied voice everywhere she went. DJs never seemed to tire of reciting the album's dedication. Romeo's Beat for Juliet, with its citation of Shakespeare. Song after song told a story that fans made their own and reconstructed for themselves about love as the highest law. She was pestered some by journalists, especially when they learned she was expecting the ill-fated artist's baby. Some clever fellow dug a little and soon DJs everywhere added, "and all these woes shall serve for sweet discourses in our time to come." Each song tore at her heart in a unique way, recollecting scenes and sounds that meant something only to her, and made her hands tremble.

Then, one day, twenty eight weeks into her pregnancy, another newly released Romeo's Beat track came on the radio just as she was getting up from her seat in the waiting room and heading in to see her obstetrician. The opening salvo of Colin's guitar pealed discordantly like Spanish church bells. They were in a little hotel room by the sea in Ribadesella. They had just come in from a long walk on the beach, and she was rinsing the sand off her feet in the bathtub.

First she heard the bells, and then the voice of her beloved singing to her. *Evermore I am with you where I found you, alleyways and street sounds, boom boom beats one sea in our hearts evermore.* She felt the little kick inside, and a surge of tears rising like a spring tide.

The kind doctor, accustomed to her emotional patients, gave her a hug and handed her a box of kleenex. Juliet sobbed in grateful relief, and then laughed at herself. The doctor spread the lubricant on her swelling belly in preparation for the ultrasound.

Juliet knew. She didn't need to be told.

"That's your little girl's heartbeat."

Romeo's Beat wasn't just alive on the radio, for others, who'd never known him. Through a sudden crack in her grief, she understood that Colin really was with her still.

By the time Gloria was born, Juliet had been restored enough to feel the entire hospital, the entire world, fall away, and herself enveloped in a warm glow of quiet joy when she held the naked newborn to her chest. Colin had died without knowing that he was a father. She had felt acutely sorrowful about this throughout her pregnancy, sorrow compounding sorrow.

But with the living, breathing baby delivered and in her arms, that sorrow was lifted, and was replaced by an unexpected balm of certainty that she was blameless and was holding him to her damp, bare chest in an even more perfect form. Precious, incandescent, magical dust, trailing clouds of glory, and gazing back up at her through newly opened deep blue eyes.

Gloria didn't just have her father's eyes. She had his ears, too. When she was as young as three, Juliet began to notice that Gloria had a habit of suddenly holding still, with her head tipped to one side. It was exactly Colin's posture when he paused to listen to some complicated layering of sound.

Raising Gloria as a single mother was hard at times, of course, and the acute sense of loss never left her completely. As mother and daughter grew stronger and more independent together, year after year, the dominant theme of their lives was joy. But that black mourning dress came over Juliet's head, feeling fresh and new, as often as it returned to a closet. Juliet knew she'd wear it, would want to wear it, always, a beloved favorite.

Gloria mourned too and began growing into her own little mourning dress the very first time she asked about the father she'd never had the chance to know. But black she refused, insisting that her favorite color was white, "like Daddy's guitar." She was a lyrical toddler, with grace and rhythm.

"Where is my Daddy?

"Daddy is gone, baby."

"But where has he gone?"

"Back to this." Juliet grabbed handfuls of the rich, dark soil that they were kneeling in, that they both loved to hold in their hands. "Where we're going. Where we came from."

"So, Daddy's here in heaven with us, momma?"

"Yes, baby. Right here with us in heaven."

Colin, so recently stricken by his own loss, had taken precautions that were unusual for such a young man. He had left a will. His sister, Clara, and Juliet were the beneficiaries of the multi-platinum *Highest Law*. Money was not a problem.

Clara was a regular feature of their lives. Her childhood memories of her brother, overlaid upon moments of uncanny recognition in Gloria, as she began to play the piano and then the guitar, gave Juliet glimpses of a much younger Colin that she could only have known in this way, even if he had been alive.

Juliet adjusted her plans and pursued her studies. Her parents and sister, and Aunt Clara, all rearranged their lives to be there for her and for Gloria. Sustainable landscapes, the persistence of native species, organic adaptation to changing environments, mutually supportive symbiotic relationships, the consistent timing of the reemergence of perennials in the spring—all her science and all her faith were intertwined.

Juliet went on talking to Colin. Out loud, some of the time, as when she'd say "oh, look!" with excitement about something Gloria had done. It seemed to others that she was just talking to herself in a natural way. But he was her constant traveling companion. She reached for him to share sights and moments that, she knew, only he would appreciate as she did.

Colin talked back to her, as she understood it, in sights and, especially, sounds. There was nothing supernatural about it. But it was never far from Juliet's mind—as she brought life from soil and watched the progress of her compost—that, in the scheme of time, there was very, very little that separated them. And in that very little that separated them, there was so much that held them together.

Juliet saw and heard through Colin's eyes and ears, and through their daughter's, as Gloria composed song after song and her career as a musician began to take flight. Juliet found the world doubled and trebled, ever sensitive to sights and soundscapes that Colin might have tried to capture and preserve, that Gloria unerringly captured and made into music that attracted fans, like moths, to her bright light by the thousands and then the hundreds of thousands.

And now, Gloria had been nominated for the Best New Artist award, and was insisting that Juliet fly with her to Los Angeles to be by her side on the red carpet and in the glaring limelight of the awards ceremony. Already, the press had begun to tell their story again. Sales figures for tracks from *Highest Law* were higher than they'd been in over a decade.

"Mom?"

No longer singing, Gloria had knelt down beside her at the edge of the garden. She had placed her own, still perfect, hands on the surface of the soil. Juliet looked at all four hands, mother's and daughter's, lined up there together side by side, and breathed in deeply. She exhaled with an enormous sense of gratitude for everything that had been packed into real time, and with gratitude for her gratitude.

"OK. I'll go to LA with you. But just this once. After that, the story is all yours."

Dust she was, and *to* dust she too would return. It all came down to the dust and to all of the magic packed into that two-letter preposition of passage.

Juliet knelt in her garden beside her daughter, their hands in the soil, where all the leaves that fall merge into one richly fertile substance, love and sunshine, particles, or one immense wave. For this, still little, while—for her forty-one trips around the sun, she had endured, had felt all of the joy, and only some small part of the grief, that a woman can feel.

www.ingramcontent.com/pod-product-compliance
Lightning Source LLC
Chambersburg PA
CBHW060649260626
47161CB00008B/3061